NIGHT CLOUDS

A COLLECTION OF SHORT STORIES

I0571712

CHRIS SYLVESTER

HUNTING CREEK PRESS

The short stories in this book are all works of fiction. All names, characters, businesses, places, events, locales, and incidents are either the products of the author's imagination or used in a fictitious manner. This book references certain living and dead celebrities and their works. These references are used only within fictional settings and situations solely created by the author. None of these celebrities or their estates are involved in any manner with this book. Any other resemblance to actual persons, living or dead, or actual events is purely coincidental.

Cover Design by MAPLE ESTUDIO

Author Photo by Mahreen Agha Photography

Copyright © 2018 Chris Sylvester

All rights reserved.

Hunting Creek Press

ISBN: 098392824X
ISBN-13: 978-0-9839282-4-9

For Lizzie, the Sylvester and Conant families, and
everyone who likes a good read

CONTENTS

ACKNOWLEDGMENTS

I am thankful to everyone that encouraged and helped me on this enjoyable journey.

For all their input and support, I would like to thank Elizabeth Kelley, my parents, and the extended Sylvester family—especially my brother Bob, a fellow short story enthusiast.

Thank you also to Mim and my network of family and friends who offered their valuable suggestions. One of the best parts of the writing process was experiencing your reactions to these stories. Thanks to all for the helpful insight that enhanced the finished product.

ENDING WITH A HUM

Journal Entry 1: September 12, Harris Spellman, Rask Pond, Maine

That goddamned humming! I don't really know how to describe it to you because there's no earthly sound that's exactly like it. The closer you get to it, the worse it hurts your ears and the more you can feel it all through your body. I hate the little yellow bastards making that terrible racket, and I wish I could do something to harm them or at least annoy them in some way ... but nobody can.

I'll try to find a way to describe that awful sound to you a little later. Just thinking about it is enough to drive me over the edge.

I might as well recap the nightmare for you from the beginning, future reader, as it could serve as a wake-up call for your generation or some other intelligent beings that reach our planet in the distant future. Actually, to be honest, I'm not really sure what could have been done to prevent this strange and awful situation. There really aren't

1

any lessons learned I can tell you as of yet. We might have been able to delay the outcome a bit, but I think the end result was always going to come about no matter what we did. Maybe your future generation or some advanced alien race can develop new technology or a plan to defeat them, but I wouldn't count on that either. I'm still trying to maintain a shred of optimism and holding out hope that someone comes up with some kind of miracle to save us.

You know what's funny? People always laughed at me for being a "prepper," but who's laughing now, huh? I've made it much longer than most have because of my frequently mocked preparation!

Well, come to think of it, the way things are going now and alone with these depressing thoughts, maybe they were right to laugh. I guess one important question you have to answer is: *Even if you can survive longer in the post-apocalyptic world, how worthwhile is it to have any extra time*? Your quality of life will certainly not be the greatest, and what happens if you don't have any company? What else will you actually have to do during that bonus survival time but reflect on the current miserable situation and your impending doom?

I'm pretty well situated to think about this topic over the next couple of weeks or maybe longer, depending on their progress. I guess I can also give you my thoughts about all the terrible things that have occurred, which might be useful for posterity. I'm willing to use some of my precious generator's fuel to power this laptop to write down my thoughts on everything. You can judge for yourselves if it has any value. I'm hoping future generations might see my musings someday, but more likely, this laptop will disappear along with everything else.

The reason I feel it's time to start getting everything

down now is that I've just begun to hear that awful humming again. I had a couple blessed weeks of quiet up here but so much for that. It's a very distant, low humming right now so that if you had a television or radio on you wouldn't hear anything, but it's definitely there. Those little yellow bastards are really coming this way.

It's amazing that you can already hear it up here in the middle of nowhere in a little DIY log cabin in the forests of northern Maine. Nothing, and I mean nothing, holds up their steady progress. Even at my retreat on this picturesque little pond, at least 30 miles from the nearest human settlement, I'm starting to hear that horrible humming again. My stomach just started cramping up, and I'm starting to sweat through my undershirt—not sure if it's a physical or a psychological reaction to hearing that unholy sound. It's probably a combination of both, and who can blame me or the scared animal inside me reacting with the proper survival instinct. Not that it's going to matter.

Lord, that's one of the worst parts of this whole stinking mess … that goddamned humming never stops.

I haven't written things down like this much in my life, and I'm surprised to find out how much it drains you. I'm also a pretty slow typist. So, I guess I'll head to bed and get back to this journal when I've got more energy. Nighttime is always the worst, as you can hear the humming the most clearly, and your brain has nothing to distract it from the situation. I haven't been sleeping too well lately. It's tough when you know that things aren't likely to get any better.

#

3

Journal Entry 2: September 13, Harris Spellman, Rask Pond

For some reason, I slept decently last night. The generous brandy nightcap probably helped matters. Let me get back to telling you the story.

The humming was really starting to get intense in the city right before I left, and it caused people to panic even more than you would imagine. I had to point my rifle at a couple of desperate souls pounding on the hood of my pickup, but luckily, I didn't have to shoot anyone. As I said earlier, I don't really know how to accurately describe the sound they make, but I'll give it a try.

People my age or older might remember the annoying tones that television stations would emit when accompanied by strange test patterns late at night. Those tones and patterns indicated the end of service for the night back when television stations weren't on the air 24/7 as they are now. The sound of the tones varied a bit by channel, but they were all pretty grating on the ears. Many more people today would recognize the distinctive noise lightsabers in the *Star Wars* movies make as they cut through the air. The current humming sounds a little like both of those sounds, but it also has these awful, constant wave-like up and down noise fluctuations that are especially irritating and seem to linger inside your head.

Also, for some reason I can't explain, you can tell that something alive is making that sound. I don't know what it is, but somehow within that strange noise, it sounds like there is a massive amount of chewing going on. I don't think that those little yellow bastards really have teeth, (Maybe they have microscopic ones or something?), but the noise they give off definitely sounds like they're eating and maybe even digesting. That humming sound gives you the creeps, for sure, no matter what is actually causing it.

I've lost the urge to write anymore today. I need to find something to distract me from this for a while.

#

Journal Entry 3: September 15, Harris Spellman, Rask Pond

I was too depressed to write anything down yesterday. It was actually tough to even get up and move around. Depression sure can take a lot out of you mentally and physically, and it's not as if I don't have a good reason to feel down. No power of positive thinking or daily affirmations are going to help at this point. However, it's a gorgeous day out there today (A day like this is why so many people visit Vacationland, folks!), and I've got some positive energy, so here goes.

Everyone was so excited when they were first discovered. I'm no science buff or technical nerd, but I'll try to explain what happened as best I can. Little did we know what was in store for all of us.

The scientists first appeared on the news to let everyone know that a good-sized asteroid, a spherical but jagged object about 30 miles in diameter, was spotted heading dangerously near our planet. The funny thing was that NASA had initially thought it was going to miss us comfortably, but they were quickly proven wrong. The sheepish looks on those eggheads' faces as they announced their "calculating error" were priceless. Later, the same scientists reported to us the startling discovery that there had to be some sort of intelligence somehow guiding the actual path of the asteroid. You can imagine the ruckus that erupted after that announcement.

The scientific analysis had at first shown the big space rock to be the normal iron-based asteroid, but they then concluded that some sort of unidentified energy source existed deep inside of it. Somehow, this energy source could sense our planet's location and had altered the object's path to intercept us. There were all kinds of speculation about how this was possible, but no decisive theory emerged. In any event, there was universal scientific agreement that some sort of intelligent life had been discovered and was making its way toward us. The reasons for their visit were unknown, but one thing was clear: everybody was nervous.

Don't ask me how (or any of the eggheads for that matter), but the energy force in the space rock also managed to slow down the speed of the object as it entered our atmosphere. The big rock then somehow separated into about 50 roughly equal pieces that scattered symmetrically around the planet. All of these different pieces landed near populated areas in open fields or in farmland with minimal impact. Teams of international scientists and researchers cordoned off the areas at the various landing sites and immediately began studying the objects. Heavily armed militaries around the world swooped in and provided airtight security at the different locations. It was the last time any of them would be useful.

For about a week or so, there was only the constant din of talking heads and scientific experts on television and online speculating about what the strange energy in the various pieces of the object could be. There seemed to be hundreds of commentators on all media sources blabbing endlessly. Who knew there were that many eggheads out there? To make it even more annoying, they all had different theories and opinions even though nobody had any evidence to base them on at that time. The main topics of discussion centered on what type of intelligent life the energy could be, and how we should try to communicate with it/them. Nobody talked too much about the danger these creatures might present, but it was definitely on everyone's minds.

The only view the public had of the big rocks was from long-range cameras, which never offered much of interest. One enterprising paparazzo tried to maneuver a drone over the rock that landed in upstate New York for some exclusive footage. The soldiers quickly shot it down before it transmitted anything interesting, and the paparazzo was arrested and publicly humiliated.

However, one intrepid researcher at the New York landing site did sell his exclusive story for untold millions. He revealed everything he knew from a blacked-out seat during a much-hyped primetime interview with one of our famous tabloid talk show hosts.

The researcher explained that the scientific team had managed to observe the strange energy inside the rock by using infrared and other advanced detection equipment, but they had not been able to analyze the energy source itself. They had also found nothing abnormal in the samples from the outer shell of the rock, which they had chipped off for analysis. The rock samples consisted mostly of iron and other common elements found in asteroids. The researcher said that his team believed that the outer shell was functioning as some sort of protective layer for the inner area, where the unique "intelligent" organisms seemed to be in some sort of dormant or hibernating state. According to the recent spikes in the readings of their energy detection devices, those organisms were clearly coming back to life in a big way. The researcher had left the landing site before things got really interesting to cash in while the asking price was at its highest.

I need a break after all that remembering and writing. I promise I'll get to the next part of the story tonight or tomorrow.

#

Journal Entry 4: September 15, Harris Spellman, Rask Pond

Okay, I can't sleep very well tonight—even worse than usual. I think it's because I'm starting to hear that humming a little bit louder now. It always seems worse at night when you can feel and hear them getting closer. So, since I'm up anyway, I might as well try to finish the next part of the story.

Things got more interesting after the researcher's primetime interview. The scientists and government officials, at least in the USA and Europe, finally decided there was no point trying to contain the already leaked preliminary findings. They arranged carefully controlled press conferences to give at least some nuggets of information to the clamoring press and public. The thing that was most noticeable at these events was how little the scientists had actually learned.

The reporters kept shouting out questions, but there were almost no clear answers. The thing that struck me at the time was that the head researcher at the New York site looked not only dumbfounded but also quite nervous. He smiled a lot and said what a wonderful thing it was to finally discover extraterrestrial life, but you could tell he was not a practiced liar. They would have been better off sending out one of the politicians or public relations officials to talk to the hungry masses of reporters.

I remember the head researcher's initial reaction when a reporter screamed out, "Is it intelligent life?" The researcher smiled, but it was definitely forced as he clumsily replied, "Ah, there are indications that it is intelligent, but, ah, we are still analyzing, ah, still trying to determine exactly … You know we've never experienced anything quite like it, uh …" I saw the momentary fear in his eyes, but then he recovered and said in a monotone, "Yes, this is a truly monumental time in human history." He again smiled weakly. The head researcher was definitely right in his analysis about what it would mean for human history. Another reporter shouted, "Are these things dangerous?" That's when the powers that be sensed they were losing control and cut off the interview. I also noticed the displeased looks on the government handlers' faces as they hustled the head researcher out of there.

I don't remember the head researcher ever leading a press conference again after that. No, after that initial press conference, it was always some dour-faced government official or public relations type that never answered any questions of importance. These spokespeople were always accomplished liars who were skilled at hiding their emotions and, more importantly, the truth. Those slimeballs were probably the type of people they should have used from the beginning to try to keep the panic to a minimum. Well, it wouldn't have mattered that much anyway after what came just a bit later.

I think I'll call it quits for tonight. It has gotten pitch black outside, and I'm exhausted enough hopefully to sleep through the distant humming. I might try some fishing tomorrow to cheer myself up a bit, so I'll get back to this when I can

#

Journal Entry 5: September 17, Harris Spellman, Rask Pond

I actually enjoyed myself fishing yesterday. I caught some nice trout and a catfish and took my time filleting and preparing them. I also found a couple crayfish hiding under some rocks near the shore. So, I gathered up a pile of freshwater mussels as well and fixed myself quite a delicious *frutti di mare* feast last night. I managed to forget about things for a little while anyway, but now I had better get back to business.

After that first uneasy week, things changed rapidly and not for the better. That was the first time we heard the humming.

Some of the research team members in New York were tired of all the restrictions and how badly they were being treated by the government handlers. One even managed to smuggle in his phone to take a video that was equal parts fascinating and terrifying. The timeframe when things started to happen was apparently identical around the world because similar videos quickly appeared online and went viral. Unfortunately, none of them were seen in time to save a lot of those first researchers.

When you look at the New York video, you can clearly see a portion of the big rock glowing brilliantly, and then it began to crack like some space giant's egg being split open to make an omelette. In the video, you can see the bright little things emerging from the rock in glowing tributaries as more cracks appeared and widened. The yellow material was a strange combination of viscous liquid and vapor as it started flowing out from the rock—kind of like molten lava with steam overhead. It quickly covered the grass in the immediate area surrounding the rock and flowed slowly but steadily toward the researchers.

One of the enthusiastic scientists probably thought he was going to make his mark on history by being the first human to make actual contact with extraterrestrial life. He walked forward and stretched out his gloved hand to touch the glowing yellow river and its accompanying mist. The researchers were all wearing those biohazard suits, but that didn't make a bit of difference. That was the first time you knew for sure there was some sort of intelligence somewhere in that yellow goop.

At first, the liquid and mist overhead flowed straight over the grass at a relatively even rate, but as soon as the creatures sensed the one courageous or foolhardy researcher walking forward and stretching his hand out, things changed. It's still unclear whether these things live in a gas or liquid form or are some unknown hybrid. All I know is the flowing and wafting yellow material near the researcher seemed to pool together into a point and purposefully engulfed the researcher's hand and arm. The yellow goop was like a moving magnet, and the scientist was an unlucky iron filing that couldn't escape its pull.

After the initial contact, the researcher didn't even have time to make a noise or move away as he was rapidly covered in the glowing material. Once they were on him, they seemed to spread out in a matter of seconds over his entire body. The next horrifying image we saw on the video looked like the special effect they use for the energizer on *Star Trek*, but Scotty wasn't beaming this crewmember anywhere safe. The researcher briefly glowed more brightly, and then his entire body, along with his useless biohazard suit, simply faded away. For an instant, you could see what looked like one of those old-fashioned silhouette photographs of the man's body and then nothing. At that exact moment, you can start to hear that awful humming for the first time.

Another team member had run toward the unfortunate pioneer to try to pull him away from the danger. However, when his colleague glowed and vanished in front of him he turned around desperately to escape, but it was too late. Now the ground and air itself seemed to be glowing, as these things spread out efficiently to capture and absorb some of the slow-footed researchers and government officials in the immediate area. This was no time to be staring in shock, but too many of them were stunned and frozen in fear and disbelief. At that point, the video becomes just a shaky blur as the researcher with the phone started to run for his life. You can hear him screaming like a maniac as he runs, swearing and praying at the same time. Luckily, he was fast enough to get away and get this video to the public. Many of his colleagues weren't so fortunate.

However, that last sentence gets back to the original question I posed in my initial journal entry. When you think of it, maybe those first victims were the lucky ones since they mercifully died right away. They at least didn't have to endure the psychological pain of the inevitable end of civilization or listen to that goddamned, never-ending humming like the rest of us.

I can't write any more tonight.

#

Journal Entry 6: September 18, Harris Spellman, Rask Pond

I started writing, but I can't think clearly today. The humming is getting louder and really distracting me. Not sure I even want to continue this journal. It's just too much right now.

#

Journal Entry 7: September 19, Harris Spellman, Rask Pond

I decided to keep writing in this journal as a big FU to the miniature space invaders and their lousy humming. I'm still alive and living my life, you little fuckers! Anyway, back to what happened.

Despite their best efforts, governments around the world couldn't contain the fear and panic produced by the New York video and similar videos worldwide. In addition, there was nothing they could do to prevent all the international television crews that were now filming the slow but steady advance of the yellow liquid and mist. Its looming presence was terrifying, as it spread out eagerly in search of more food, energy, or whatever you want to call it.

You can probably guess what happened after that. Things deteriorated pretty much as you would imagine when the world is coming to an end. At first, there was hope that all the nations of the world could come up with some heroic way of stopping the "yellow hordes," as someone dubbed them. Unfortunately, unlike in all of our favorite movies, nothing stopped them. Nothing.

The world's great military powers tried every type of conventional and experimental weapon, every type of chemical and biological agent, every type of hazardous and non-hazardous material, extreme freezing and melting, lasers, and even sonic and photovoltaic weapons. No, nuclear weapons didn't faze them either.

There were also valiant attempts by psychics who claimed they could use their telekinetic abilities to halt their advance. Various-sized groups from organized religions and enthusiastic new age types tried using the power of prayer and spiritual energy.

Nothing worked. Nothing even slowed them up in any significant way. The yellow hordes kept advancing steadily, and that awful humming kept getting louder.

We all numbly watched the increasingly desperate news reports until the major power stations succumbed. The big networks used animated maps to track the continuing spread of the yellow hordes. It was a horrifying and stunning display, but you just couldn't take your eyes off those colorful maps and the ever-expanding real estate of the yellow bastards. It was like watching a twisted version of the ball drop on New Year's Eve in Times Square, but nobody was going to be kissing or partying when this countdown finished.

Government officials evacuated people, animals, and important materials and objects away from the destructive path as best as they could, but it was only a temporary reprieve. Ultimately, there were no safe zones. The scary thing was that these nasty buggers consumed or absorbed everything in their path. They seemed to prefer organic material, but they would also happily eat through any inorganic material to get there. Some materials took a little longer to be absorbed but not enough time to matter.

My brain is fried after that depressing recap, so I'll try writing some more tomorrow.

#

Journal Entry 8: September 20, Harris Spellman, Rask Pond

Let me fill you in on some of the last things that happened before I headed up here.

One of the last television reports I watched had a sad-looking evolutionary biology expert in studio postulating his theories about the yellow hordes. Nobody ever did determine exactly how big the organisms were. It was also unclear whether they were an integral part of the yellow liquid and gas, or if they merely traveled through them to get to the matter they would consume. As far as I know, nobody ever found any way to study them up close and personal without getting absorbed.

The expert on television was quite impressed with the yellow hordes, saying that they most likely had existed throughout space for billions of years. He speculated that they even might have originated in another universe or dimension. He also theorized that there could be multiple groups of their species wreaking havoc in all the distant corners of the known and unknown universe or universes. In any event, he said they seemed to have evolved into indestructible life forms that don't die. They feed or regenerate at opportune time periods and then hibernate in asteroids and other unknown inorganic vessels for millions or billions of years until they reach another suitable planet with more organic life to consume. He even smiled grimly as he noted that they might represent the apex of intelligent life since they absorbed all other life forms into their communal yellow goop. There was no way to measure how intelligent they really were, but it was clear they had proven to be the dominant species as the ultimate survivors. They would soon conquer our planet and add us to their ever more powerful energy source, containing what had to be countless other civilizations.

The expert theorized that they would absorb all life on our planet and then move down into the Earth's core itself. He explained that they would then likely hibernate again for another long period, but nobody could predict what would happen with them once the Sun eventually consumed our planet in the distant future.

He then described another possibility with a wry and disturbing smile saying, "However, at some time well before that point, the yellow hordes might have reformed some sections of the Earth into asteroid-like objects and propelled themselves safely toward the next solar system. Maybe this process allows them to reproduce and form new asteroid containers if that is even necessary. In any case, at some point they will initiate a new lifecycle and continue to do what they do so well at the next unlucky planet."

In short, he told us nobody could say for sure what would eventually happen, and none of us would ever know. The only thing that seemed definite from his explanation was that those little bastards were basically immortal.

When the stressed out newscaster, who had given up on blow-drying her hair or using much makeup, had asked him how long he estimated until the yellow hordes absorbed all life on Earth, he shrugged his shoulders, scratched his scruffy beard, and said, "Probably six months for most of the planet. I would estimate that they will get to the most remote life forms, including the single-celled organisms in the deep trenches of the oceans and in the polar ice caps, within about a year. Hard to say exactly, but they are remarkably steady in their progress." His last sentence was spoken in a strange whisper. I couldn't stand looking at the vacant expression on his face anymore, so I turned off the television. There was nothing more he could tell us anyway.

I should also note that there had been some hope that maybe the yellow buggers didn't like fresh or salt water since they first set down exclusively on land. However, this hope was quickly dashed after video reports came from some big island, (Madagascar maybe?), which showed the yellow hordes moving steadily from the now glowing yellow landmass into the ocean to join up with their fellow hordes in Africa and India. The fishes wouldn't be spared either, folks. People said the glow in the ocean was beautiful to witness, and it did look fascinating on video. The eyewitnesses said it was more stunning than any sunset on water they had ever experienced. I guess I could understand that observation, as long as you didn't know that the source of that beautiful sight was consuming everything on the planet, and if it wasn't accompanied by that bone-chilling humming.

I watched another desperate news report that talked about wealthy survivalist types buying cruise ships or sealing off underground bunkers to avoid the yellow hordes for as long as possible. They also reported on some creative folks trying to organize a last outpost using blimps and balloons tethered together in a makeshift cloud city. Clever, yes, but you still have to come back down to the ground eventually to get more supplies, which would mean game over.

I think the last members of our species will be the astronauts up in the various space stations orbiting the Earth. Wonder how long they'll last without being resupplied? What an amazing view they'll have when the whole planet is glowing gold.

The last unconfirmed reports on the president and Congress said they were sheltering deep in that NORAD bunker under some mountain out west. However, it doesn't matter how deep they go, or how far they try to run away on land or sea, the yellow hordes will eventually get to all of them.

I also saw a few surreal news reports showing groups of people holding hands and lying down peacefully in fields, yards, or roads with family and friends as the yellow hordes steadily approached. Some of the people must have taken sedatives or some other medication beforehand because they didn't look panicked. In contrast, most of them seemed somewhat relieved as they were quickly absorbed.

In the end, after a little inner debate, I figured I might as well use my cabin since I spent all that time, effort, and money preparing for the end of the world. However, part of me had an uneasy feeling that maybe those people now at peace had the right idea.

I feel used up after all that writing. It might take me a couple of days to get back to this.

#

Journal Entry 9: September 22, Harris Spellman, Rask Pond

I swam and fished the last couple of days and it wasn't bad. I felt relatively normal for a short time. You can't actually hear that horrible humming underwater. I wish I had a scuba tank and endless air tanks so that I could stay underwater all day and night. Well, let me get you updated on what happened next.

Those stories I described were the last news reports I saw or heard before I packed up and headed to my prepper getaway up north. At this point, I don't think any power plants or television stations still exist to give any more reports.

What I knew when I left was that the yellow hordes were coming at me from New York on one side and from the Atlantic Ocean on the other, after sweeping steadily through Europe and the UK.

I armed myself to the teeth and drove up here with almost no stops. I was surprised at how little traffic there was, but I still stayed on the side roads to be as safe as possible. I guess most people either had given up by then or had already reached their last holdout positions. As I mentioned earlier, after I got here, I had a couple of weeks of refreshing tranquility. Unfortunately, my peace and quiet ended about ten days ago when I began to write things down.

Now you are up-to-date with me in my journal about the last gasps of the planet Earth. I'm writing some information below about my current living situation that you might find interesting.

I prepped well and have enough regular and freeze-dried food and supplies to live comfortably for ten years in my log cabin. Unfortunately, I won't get to use most of my carefully hoarded provisions. I also have plenty of guns and ammo as well as barricades to discourage visitors, which isn't going to help me at all in this situation. In addition, I have a decent amount of fuel for my generator, water from the pond to drink and bathe in, and wood all around me to fuel my stove for heating and cooking. I also have a well-stocked library of books, DVDs, music CDs, and this laptop for my entertainment. I'm an only child whose parents are long dead, and my wife divorced me five years back. Basically, I didn't have anyone to rescue and bring up here with me.

I am now thinking about getting into my pickup and heading down the lumber company road to that mom-and-pop variety store near the turnoff about 30 miles back. There was a cute woman at that store who smiled at me a little as I filled up my gas containers and bought some beef jerky and an old copy of *People* magazine. So sweet and what a body! Hell, maybe she would be interested in hanging on with me as long as possible up here at my prepper's paradise. I'll even let her write her thoughts down in this journal as well.

You know, even if that sweet woman was married with a family, I would offer my hospitality to all of them. If I can't find any people back there, maybe I can rescue a stray cat or dog to keep me company. At this point, I would even take a gerbil! Anything's better than being alone, especially during this mother of all clusterfucks. However, I'm hesitant to go back that way because I just don't want to be any closer to that damned humming for as long as humanly possible. I'd better make a decision on a potential ride that way soon since I'm not exactly sure how much longer it's going to be doable.

One thing I've noticed is that there are no mosquitoes around anymore, and I don't see hardly any other insects either. One very small blessing of this nightmare is not having to deal with the usual swarms of what the locals call the Maine state bird. The black flies that come out in June are pretty nasty up here, too. They all seem to have retreated somewhere even more remote. Wonder how long it's going to take for the little bugs to meet their end? The flying ones might last a bit longer, but everything has to land eventually, right? They're all going to be swarmed over themselves real soon by something a lot nastier.

I've watched a bunch of my DVD movies and classic television collections, which were okay, but I was surprised to find out that I actually miss reality shows. I didn't even watch them much before this whole mess. Now I guess I'm feeling nostalgic for having the time to be interested in absurd things like that.

For a while there, my shortwave radio had been getting some signals, although they weren't very clear. Most of the transmissions I could make out were in foreign languages. I've tried contacting other prepper types I know around the world a bunch of times, but no soap. Lately, I've only been getting static. What I wouldn't give to just hear another live human voice.

#

Journal Entry 10: September 25, Harris Spellman, Rask Pond

What total bullshit! It's really hitting home now. Nothing is changing, and it's not going to be any different tomorrow. Why couldn't anybody on this entire planet figure something out, dammit? All the trillions of dollars spent on weapons and scientific research throughout our existence and those morons can't come up with anything to save us?

If this is really how it's going to end for us, it then begs the big question: *What was the point of it all?* I can't even come up with a half-assed answer to that one.

I'm thinking of throwing this stupid laptop into the pond.

#

Journal Entry 11: September 27, Harris Spellman, Rask Pond

So, anyhow, this will be one of my last entries. I'm wearing earbuds all the time now to try to block that damned humming, but it's hopeless. The noise somehow always manages to get through, and I can also feel the sound vibrations from the ground pulsing through my entire body. I never made it back to the variety store to pick up that cute woman or even any stray animals. After driving a few miles down the lumber road, I could already see the bright glow in the distance. The intensity of the humming and the glowing made it clear that there wasn't any earthly life left where that variety store had been.

This may sound funny, but I dug out a little area on the beach and filled it with water to make a small man-made pond like you see for Koi and goldfish in some people's backyards. I put some crayfish and catfish that I caught into my little handmade pond and have spent a decent amount of time observing them. I surrounded it with rocks and wood to keep the water and my little buddies in there. I found a little frog and put him in there, too, but he escaped sometime during the night. My cute little pond keeps my mind occupied, and I've got to admit I actually like the company, such as it is. Kind of pathetic I know, but you try to think of ways to keep your mind off a situation like this!

I'm thinking about building a makeshift shelter on that little island in the middle of the real pond to buy a little more time, but is it really worth it? I figure I've got about a week left here in my cabin before their arrival. My island retreat might extend things another few days if I'm lucky.

You know what? Even though the quality of life will be virtually non-existent, I am going to head to that island. What the hell, right? I've trained all my life to survive during the end of the world as long as possible, so I might as well put my money where my mouth is and go balls out to the end. I guess that answers that original question for you, huh? At least for people like me anyway. I'm pretty sure I'm in the minority group with my answer, judging by what I've witnessed over the last couple of months.

I really don't like freeze-dried food, nuts, crackers, and such, but that's primarily what I'm going to have to subsist on for as long as it takes for them to get to me out there. Maybe I'll bring some hot dogs with me and have a weenie roast out on my island the first night. Might be the last weenie roast ever taking place on the planet, so why not? I might as well use up the marshmallows and chocolate, too. I'm thinking weenies and s'mores won't be a bad last real meal for the condemned man.

The bright glow and the humming are now coming from all sides. I can feel it pulsing through my eyes now. Just awful. It's not really coming fast but steadily, always steadily.

I'm trying to think of the best place to store this laptop where it might have a chance to avoid being consumed. There's a hill about a half mile away that has a gigantic boulder on top of it. That awe-inspiring boulder was left there by the glaciers of the last ice age. We won't be having any more of those in the foreseeable future. I'm hoping that if I climb up my rope ladder and put the laptop up there it might not be absorbed, but it's really only a faint hope.

#

Journal Entry 12: September 30, Harris Spellman, Rask Pond

I didn't get a chance to get to that big boulder with my laptop. Those damned things always move just a little faster than you think. I probably could have made it there, but it would have been fifty-fifty getting back. I don't believe it would have made a difference anyway because I think most rocks are being consumed, too. Maybe they are eating the moss and other small creatures on and inside the rocks, or they might enjoy dining on some minerals, too. Who knows? A mad dash is just not worth the risk in any case, and this journal writing stuff has kind of grown on me. I'll keep the entries going as long as I can, but it will depend on how long this battery lasts after my generator gets snuffed out.

Now I'm getting my final thoughts written down for nobody really other than myself. I'm not a deep thinker, but something just occurred to me. Nobody had ever imagined or forecast this bizarre and somewhat embarrassing ending for us. All the religions loved to preach their grand versions of Armageddon with angels, demons, floods, pestilence, fire and brimstone, etc. Scientists theorized about the end via climate change, food shortages, plagues, and even alien invasions from little green men in flying saucers. There have also been feature movies made about possible extinction level events from asteroids like the one that wiped out the dinosaurs, but I've never heard of anything like this scenario. It just proves the old adage that truth is stranger than fiction after all. I just laughed out loud thinking about the whole absurdity of humanity's end: We're all going to end up as food for some little yellow space creatures.

Wonder how much energy our planet is going to add to the ever-growing yellow hordes? Who knows how many other civilizations we'll be joining in that yellow goop, right? What a way for us and all those other beings to end! How did they deal with it on their worlds, I wonder? There were probably some little green guys like me holding out as long as possible, but who knows? Nobody will ever be able to read or know about any of their last thoughts on our shared awful experience either.

If there is a God or creator, I can't help but ask him: *Why did it have to be like this?* Is this some form of cruel punishment or just the natural order of things? Should we be taking this personally or not? We're not all bad enough to deserve this fate, are we? Couldn't he have let some of the best people survive? I don't even include myself in that select group, believe me!

I released the crayfish and catfish in my little man-made pond back into the real pond. They were all swimming and acting crazy because they could really feel and hear that damned humming. Hey, it's not going to buy them much more time, but every minute is precious, right? At least they'll be free, and they can try to stay away from those yellow bastards until the very end. Godspeed, my little buddies!

#

Final Journal Entry: October 2, Harris Spellman, Rask Pond

I'm heading out to the island today. I'll have just enough time to get out there if I leave in the next half hour. They'll get to my generator probably within the next hour or so. I've already got my trusty Old Town canoe loaded and ready, but I don't want to cut it any closer than that. I'll bring the laptop with me, but I don't think the battery will last that long. Maybe I'll grab a pen and some paper and keep writing until the end out there. Or, maybe I'll just try to relax, meditate, and think about other things until it's over. How much more is there really left to say? Oh well, we'll see how I feel once I get settled on my island.

Man is that humming loud now. It seems to be pulsing throughout my entire body day and night. It's impossible to sleep, so I think I'm having hallucinations. I thought I saw yellow deer, raccoons, and bears walking by my cabin this morning, but it's probably just my mind playing tricks on me. I swear my heart is now beating in rhythm to the humming whether I want it to or not. The glow is blinding as they're all around me. Every tree as far as the eye can see is gone, and all the hills are painted bright yellow. I don't even get much relief underwater at this point, and I haven't seen any fish lately. No idea where they're trying to hide, but it won't do them any good. Well, it might buy them an extra day or two, so who am I to criticize.

As I said earlier, I'll probably have another few days to ponder this situation some more depending on how quickly these nasty things get across my little pond to my final holdout.

Wonder if it's going to hurt at all?

As I described earlier, I've got a decent little library in my cabin. In some of the stories and poems I've found about the end times, writers much more skilled than I am use phrases like *ending with a bang* or *ending with a whimper*. It turns out, to everyone's surprise, the world, and everything and everybody in it, are all going to be ending with a hum.

NIGHT CLOUDS

FINDING GALILEE

There were only a handful of them left now. Most of the Marines in his squad either had been killed earlier or were too wounded to fight. Gunnery Sergeant John Brophy had been through many tough situations in this endless war, but none as desperate as this one.

Okinawa was turning out to be worse than any of the other miserable islands, and that was saying something. The Japs had fought tough before, but somehow they had ratcheted it up to another, almost super-human level. He and his men were used to *banzai* charges and suicide attacks, but now more of the bastards seemed to be getting into the act, and they didn't seem to go down as easily as before. For another fun wrinkle, Japanese civilians from the island were getting involved. They were helping the Jap soldiers out with reconnaissance and Intel, and unwilling accomplices were being used as human shields in brazen attacks on the thousands of U.S. Marines and Army soldiers trying to take this mud-drenched shithole.

What made things on Okinawa even more terrible than the previous islands were the sheer size of it, the ferocity of the defense, the Japanese civilians, the horrible rainy weather and mud that made the difficult terrain even worse, and yet another new level of fanaticism from these crazies—*kamikaze* pilots. Brophy had heard of sporadic *kamikaze* attacks before but never of this magnitude. The ferocious attacks were coming in continuous waves with hundreds of planes trying to hit the Navy support ships near the island. These attacks were killing and wounding a lot of men and making the resupply of personnel and materials difficult. That made things worse for everyone.

With all these complicating factors hindering the overall invasion effort, Brophy and the remnants of his squad were already facing severe supply shortages before their current predicament. Now things had gotten even worse for them.

He and his squad had been forced to pull out and regroup after a massive nighttime attack on the entire division frontline two nights before. The attack had eventually been thwarted, but there had been high US casualties and a lot of confusion. The battle lines had also shifted, and Brophy and his men found themselves behind enemy lines in an isolated sector with no access to their already limited supplies. Most importantly, they didn't have any water nor barely any ammunition.

They had managed to find an abandoned, half-destroyed hut close to a small hill, and they were occupying it without the nearby Japs realizing it. Luckily, most of the action was taking place toward the center of the island, a good five miles distant, so there were relatively few enemy troops in this area of the Japanese lines. Brophy and his men had figured out that the closest current US position was about a half mile from where they were located, at a well-defended ridgeline. There was also a decent footpath they could use to get back to the base of the ridgeline. They would be safe if they could make it there, as friendly units were dug in around the area.

However, the footpath went right by the nearby enemy-occupied hill, where there was a small detachment of well-armed Japs. At the base of the hill, there was a little spring and a waterfall with fresh water, which they were guarding. There were probably at least two dozen of them in the area, and they had at least one heavy machine gun covering the spring. To make matters worse, there were also explosive booby traps in place for anyone who walked by without knowing their way around. Somehow, Brophy and his men would have to get by these defenses to get water and to make it out of there alive.

"Whatcha thinkin', Gunny?" asked Red Thompson, the teenage rifleman from Arkansas in his distinctive drawl. We gonna make a play for that water soon? I'm so thirsty I could lick the sweat off a hawg."

"I'm sure that 'hawg' would be grateful, too, Red," said Martinelli in his nasal Jersey accent as he cleaned his BAR. "I'm so fuckin' thirsty I'd even lick the sweat off yer balls at this point!"

Brophy smiled and replied with a question to Navy Corpsman Paul "Doc" Leiderman, "What do you think, Doc? Would the hog sweat or ball sweat work best to cut down our thirst?" He tried to keep a straight face as he continued, "Hey, you're the medical expert and are always warning us about dehydration and trench foot and the like. C'mon, give us your two cents!"

"Well, Gunny, it is my esteemed medical opinion that hog sweat would be preferable in this instance."

"Why's that, Doc?"

"Because you can also get some nutrition from that hog's sweat ... and think of that bacony flavor! You also won't have to worry about swallowing any of the vermin that are living comfortably on the back of Red's balls."

The men cracked up at that, although they still made sure to keep their voices low.

"Your watch, Red," Brophy said and then turned to Doc and pointed to the back of the hut. "Step into my office for a second."

"What's the latest?" Brophy whispered with a nod of his head toward the two seriously wounded men lying on the dirt floor of the hut.

"Miller is hanging in there, but I'm not liking the color around those wounds on his arm. If we don't get him help soon, he'll lose his arm and probably his life in short order." He frowned and continued his depressing report, "Warczek hasn't regained consciousness since that mortar shell exploded. I think he might be in a coma of some sort, but his vital signs are stable for the moment. But, if we don't get him medicine and fluids soon, it will all be over. As a matter of fact, that goes for the rest of us as well."

Brophy nodded his head grimly. They had pooled their water and rations and given as much as possible to the wounded men. The rest of them had been nicked up pretty good in various ways. It was a miracle that any of them had survived the initial attack. Brophy also knew that nobody was coming to help them. Command had already given them up for dead along with all the others in their unit. They had no radio to tell anyone differently. Tonight would have to be the night they shot the moon and tried to make it back to safety.

Brophy figured that, at a minimum, they would need to kill the Jap sentries near the spring just to get some water. Otherwise, they wouldn't have the strength to make it back to the friendly ridgeline. The problem was that if anything went wrong, and the Japs around the hill were alerted to their presence, they would quickly be outnumbered and outgunned. All they had was the element of surprise, and that would have to be enough.

Brophy was the least hurt among the walking wounded, so he would be taking the risky lead role in their longshot plan. He called Red, Gantry, and Martinelli over.

"Okay boys, here's the best plan as far as I see it. Me and Gantry will head over there and take out the sentries quickly and quietly. If things go okay, I'll send Gantry back with water to rejuvenate everyone as much as possible before we make the final push through. Once we're ready, we'll make a quiet run with Doc and Miller carrying or dragging Warczek and the rest of us providing cover."

He now looked each man in the eye as he addressed him, "If the Japs see or hear us and come after us, Martinelli, I want you to focus your BAR on any machine gun crews, otherwise we're finished. Red, you can pick off any snipers or stragglers coming down from the hill above. Gantry and me will take care of whoever is right in the area. I think if we can get past them quickly and get going down that path we've got a chance." He paused for a second then added, "Even if there is some contact, I don't think a lot of their buddies will waste their time and resources coming after us. The main action, thank God, is toward the center of the island, so that's where they'll be keeping their attention." Brophy hoped they believed that last statement more than he did. He needed them to be focused and optimistic to give them any chance.

Martinelli piped up with his doubts as always, "Gunny, this seems like a stretch. We don't even know how many of them there are over there. We're comfortable and safe all holed up here. Maybe we should wait a bit longer—I just know they'll come lookin' for us."

"You're right, Martinelli. There could be a whole Jap division full of *banzai*-charging fanatics all over and around that hill. Tojo himself could be just waiting to lead them into battle and aiming to personally chop your head off with his favorite *katana* sword!" Brophy smiled a bit then finished. "And we're going to do our best to get by them before they even know what happened. If things don't work out, we're going to take a lot of those bastards with us. Anyway, it beats dying of thirst in this stinky, sweaty hut, doesn't it fellas?"

"You said it, Gunny!" Red exclaimed. "We'll take 'em all out even if there are a hundred yellow shitbirds waiting!" Brophy knew he could always count on Red, who looked up to him almost like a father figure. He was only 29, but he seemed much older and more mature to the 19-year-old Red.

Brophy quickly surveyed the others and knew they had all reluctantly agreed. Gantry, the Ohio farm boy who rarely spoke, just nodded his head slowly. Martinelli closed his eyes, looked slowly down at his feet, and nodded begrudgingly. Doc looked Brophy in the eye and said quietly, "I don't see any other way for those wounded boys or us at this point."

As they waited for it to get a bit later, they sat quietly in a circle in the hut. The jokes weren't flowing anymore as the time for action approached. Most of them kept their thoughts to themselves, and some looked at snapshots from home.

Brophy took a long look at a crumpled photo of his wife Lorraine, whom he had hurriedly married before he shipped out almost three years before. He didn't look at her picture often enough because it was just too painful. The love and beauty that radiated from her picture just didn't seem to belong in the stinking hellholes where they had to struggle and fight to survive.

In the distance, the men could hear the usual artillery and mortar salvos going back and forth as well as sporadic automatic weapon and sniper fire. There were also some occasional yells and moans. None of that fazed them anymore. They had all seen far too much at this point.

Brophy thought back to seeing his first dead Jap sprawled in some scrub brush on the 'Canal. He had been trying to find someplace to quietly take a leak in peace when he came upon that awful surprise. The man had been killed months earlier and was badly decomposed. Insects and land crabs were crawling over him and picking at his bones through his tattered uniform. Brophy had to fight hard not to puke in front of the others when he returned.

When he saw his first men blown to red, frothy fragments in front of him on Tarawa, he did lose his breakfast, all over the landing craft's already slick deck. He quickly regained his composure and killed for the first time that day. Since then he had taken care of Japs with his carbine, sidearm, bayonet, Ka-Bar, shovel, and even his bare hands. He had even finished one poor bastard off with his helmet.

Brophy had also frequently ordered Marines with grenades, satchel charges, and flamethrowers to incinerate Japs in bunkers and other fortifications. He never understood why those fools didn't surrender when facing that terrible end. That horrible stench, a pungent mixture of gasoline and burning human flesh, was the worst of all the awful smells he had experienced on the battlefield. You didn't ever get used to any of it, but you did become numb. Otherwise, you would go insane, and some men certainly did.

Fortunately, the moon and stars weren't out tonight, which slightly increased the chance that their plan would work. Red was always talkative, and this night was no different.

"Ya know, this dark night reminds me of a sermon I heard when I was a boy back home," he began with his usual enthusiasm.

"Oh, gawd!" Martinelli groaned. "No more holy roller shit. Not tonight, please!"

"Well, it was about finding Galilee and—"

Martinelli cut him off saying, "Finding what 'Lee?' The only 'Lee' I want to find again is a cute dame in Honolulu named Rosalie. Remember that brown-skinned beauty I met working at the canteen, guys? *Che bella figliola!* What a dish!"

Red ignored him and continued his story with a hushed and somber voice, "A twister had just gone through the town next door. It killed a few people and flattened some buildings. For some reason, the next day and night were really still and dark just like tonight. Some people from our town and the one that got hit organized a memorial service down at the First Lutheran Church. He paused for a few seconds as he tried to remember the story. Nobody interrupted.

"My folks made us attend services there every Sunday, usually in the evening, and I don't particularly remember any of the sermons except for that there one after the twister. Reverend Lansing was always pretty mild-mannered and kept his sermons short and to the point. Not that evening, I'll tell ya." The men remained silent as Red closed his eyes and thought back to that night.

"He came in and looked disheveled and confused through the first readings and such. Then he wiped his brow, got up out of his chair, and gave the most energetic sermon I ever heard. He kept talking about 'the will of the Lord' and that human suffering was all part of his glorious plan. He spent a lot of time talking about that guy in the bible who everything bad happened to—Joab, I think his name was? Or something like that."

Red was silent for a moment, and even the usual din of automatic weapons clattering in the distance stopped. He continued in the same measured voice, "At the end, he talked about the importance of everyone finding Galilee. I guess that's the name of that area over in the Holy Land where Jesus gave all those lessons to the people and did all those miracles and some such. I think it's also where he wandered around after rising up from the dead after they crucified him on the cross." Red paused for a few seconds then continued, "The reverend explained that Galilee is the place where his followers knew their faith in Jesus and God's plan was justified and that nothing could hurt them now. They were all saved, and they would realize eternal life no matter what happened to them on Earth. He then said it was up to all of us to find our Galilee here on Earth, realize our faith in Jesus and God's plan, serve and sacrifice for our fellow men, and understand that salvation awaited us. The important thing was that we just needed to understand that everything that happened was all the will of the Lord." Red paused for about 10 seconds as he reflected back on that night. Brophy thought that he appeared to have aged 20 years during the telling of the story.

Red then continued with a serious voice that seemed strange coming from him. "It was an amazing sermon, and you could have heard a pin drop in that church when he finished up, I tell ya. People then started to sob in a strange mixture of sadness and joy. I'm not ashamed to say that even my old tough as nails pappy had tears streaming down his sun-burnt cheeks."

Red bowed his head in silence for a few seconds before he continued, "And then, about a minute after he finished speaking, Reverend Lansing just stepped right down from that pulpit and walked slowly up the middle aisle of the church toward the front door. His hair was uncombed, and he had a faraway look in his eyes and an unusual, crooked smile on his face. He walked silently by everyone without a word, and his expression never changed. He just looked somehow like he wasn't with us anymore. Nobody had the nerve to speak to him or shake his hand. He just opened the main door and walked out into the darkness. He left the door wide open after he went out, so I can clearly remember that the sky was similar to tonight. There were no moon or stars, and it was so quiet that you could hear the people in the church softly weeping."

The battlefield around them remained silent as Red

continued, "We all heard later that night that Reverend Lansing's wife and two small children had been killed when their house was flattened by that twister. He was apparently off ministering to a dying woman at the local clinic and had to seek shelter there. None of us ever saw him again after that night. We heard that he was transferred to another parish in Texas or somewhere." Red paused again as if he were finished talking and then added, "Well, at least he found his Galilee anyway."

Nobody in the hut spoke for a bit, and then Martinelli said half-heartedly, "Boy, Red, that's comforting. At least we won't have to worry about getting killed by a goddamned twister tonight. *Madonna mia*! What a depressing story!"

Red answered quickly, "Well, I take some comfort in it. If you've got Jesus in your life, there's nothing that you can't handle! Right, Gunny?"

Red looked at Brophy hoping for his support. Brophy acknowledged the power of the message, but he quickly refocused the men back to their mission saying, "Red, it sure seems like your reverend found his Galilee. God bless him for trying to help others learn some powerful messages even during the worst day of his life. Now, c'mon fellas, let's all say a quick prayer for the rest of us in the here and now, and get ready to go."

About a half hour after Red's story, Brophy and Gantry had managed to quickly and silently kill three Jap sentries with their knives. It looked like the Japs had been drinking some, as they were half-asleep at their posts near the spring. Brophy wondered if it was maybe some Jap festival time or if the men were just trying to numb themselves from the usual wartime misery. He was glad it was easier to kill them, but a dark part of him wished that they had been more awake to feel the pain of their deaths. God, how he hated them all and what they had done to so many of his men. Anger rose up in him as he thought about all the innocents that had died because of their damned war and their subhuman behavior. As always, he put the hate away because he had to concentrate on his mission.

Brophy and Gantry drank heartily from the spring and filled up as many canteens as possible. Brophy then sent Gantry back to the others with the precious water and kept watch on the hill for more Japs.

After about 15 minutes, and with their terrible thirst slaked, his squad began to carry out the rest of the plan.

Doc and Miller had managed to move Warczek up near the spring, and they were about to head down the path toward friendly lines. Martinelli and Red were covering them. Gantry was walking quietly toward Brophy with a slight smile on his face about to take point when everything went to hell. A Japanese soldier had suddenly appeared out of the darkness, probably to relieve one of the sentries, and bumped smack into Gantry. Both men gasped as they realized what was happening. The Japanese soldier then started to scream for help while Gantry tried desperately to cover his mouth and knife him at the same time. During their frantic struggle, they tripped over a rock and fell on top of one of the explosive booby traps to the right of the spring.

After the deafening explosion, Brophy realized that now they really had to haul ass, and he screamed at Doc and Miller to get moving. He also ordered Martinelli to spray the machine gun nest. Everyone followed orders like the well-oiled machine they were. Martinelli wiped out the two guys who had popped up in the machine gun nest, Red picked off a couple coming down the hill, and Brophy sprayed the base of the hill where the Japanese soldier had appeared earlier, killing a couple more. It seemed like they might have a chance.

Then Brophy saw a fresh group of Japanese soldiers coming around the hill right near his location behind a small boulder. The Japs set up a machine gun only about ten feet from him and started firing at Martinelli and the others. Brophy managed to kill a few more near the machine gun, but there were too many for him to handle. He saw Martinelli go down after a sustained burst, and now he realized he had no automatic weapons support. Red tried his best to keep the Japanese soldiers down, but he was pinned down himself by their sheer numbers and superior fire. Doc, Miller, and the unconscious Warczek lay sprawled behind a couple of medium-sized boulders closer to the start of the footpath. They were agonizingly close to the path that would bring them back to friendly territory, but they were trapped and couldn't move an inch.

The Japanese fire was deafening and ferocious as it swept over the Americans' positions. Brophy recognized that the Japs would soon kill or capture everyone, and he knew full well what they did with prisoners. He realized there was only one play left, or they were all finished.

Hey, he said to himself, *nobody said finding Galilee was going to be easy*. Brophy felt like crying as he thought briefly of Lorraine, but he quickly focused on what he had to do. He looked down at his satchel, which had a grenade and an anti-tank mine in it, and placed it forward around his neck. He then climbed up on the boulder and sprayed the last of his carbine's clip into the surprised enemy below. Brophy managed to get one of the machine gun crew, but another soldier quickly took his place. The rest of the Japanese soldiers now focused their fire on him.

He felt bullets hit his arm, and one grazed his head. In agony, he spread his arms out wide getting ready to jump and bullets ripped through both arms and smashed into his body. He gathered what little strength he had left and jumped as far as he could. He landed directly on one of the explosive booby traps located between the spring and the Japanese.

The last thing Brophy heard was Red yelling, "Gunny, nooooooo, don't do it, we can stop—!"

The explosion was deafening and powerful and made short work of the dozen or so Japanese soldiers left. Then there was only the horrible wartime smell of explosives and death accompanied by a strange, oddly peaceful silence.

Doc and Miller quickly emerged from their hiding place and struggled to move Warczek's limp body. Red stumbled by in a daze, and Doc grabbed him hard by the arm and yelled, "Help us carry Warczek, and let's get the hell out of here!"

Red had tears in his eyes and pleaded with Doc, "But, what about Gunny? Oh no. Please, no. I can't do it. I can't …" He started to cry and then had trouble breathing as he sobbed violently.

"Move it now, Red," Doc ordered sternly, "or this is all for nothing!"

Red looked one last time at the awful carnage, wiped his tears away, and then turned quickly to help the others make it down the path to salvation.

THE BEAST

Bill Schenk had a big problem. If he didn't overcome this problem, he soon wouldn't have to worry about dealing with problems ever again. His friend and coworker, Jack Maloney, had already reached that non-worrying state, as he was lying nearby on the muddy ground dead from a shotgun blast.

Schenk had faced many relatively big problems in his life, such as a sexual harassment lawsuit and a tense situation with some IRS officials, and he had overcome them all. However, he had never faced a situation where his life was in danger, and it most certainly was today.

His problematic situation was surreal and simple: he was alone and lying seriously wounded and exposed in a rural area of India where tigers and other predators roamed. He had no access to first aid or any type of medicine, and there was nobody around to help him.

How had he gotten here? he was now asking himself while he calmly tried to settle his breathing and ignore the excruciating pain in his face, leg, and side. It didn't help that the temperature was well in the 90s even though it was late at night, and he was completely drenched in sweat. Some kind of crawling insects were biting him on his exposed skin and even seemed to be burrowing into his wounds. What struck Schenk most, during what was easily the worst moment of his life, was how clearly he was hearing and sensing the strange creatures around him. Some sort of primeval survival instinct had arisen in him while he lay on the ground taut with tension.

Up until now, life had been quite a good ride for Schenk. He was 37 and a rising sales executive for a multinational corporation headquartered just outside of Washington, DC. He wasn't conventionally good looking, but he had a good physique (honed through dedicated hours of pick-up basketball and intense workouts at the gym), and he knew how to dress and act to succeed in business and in the social jungle. He also knew how to ingratiate himself with the other winners in the office whether they be on the way up or already established. His aggressive nature also worked well with many of the opposite sex, who often found his sarcastic sense of humor and overall arrogance alluring. He had enjoyed many conquests and much personal satisfaction without the need for relationships, which suited him perfectly. Most of the women he met and bedded quickly understood the type of man he was. The few naïve ones who tried to get closer to him were simply ignored.

Although Schenk had lived an overall rewarding life in his eyes, he had dealt with some awkward situations that might have derailed a less accomplished man. A couple of years back he had flirted with a hot new marketing intern, who had initially responded warmly to his advances.

Something about her youth and innocence had made her even more appealing to Schenk. During a late night of proposal work, he had decided to take their flirting to the next level in the break room. However, the attractive intern had inexplicably had second thoughts and rebuffed him.

Angered by this rare rejection, Schenk decided to spread some embarrassing sexual rumors about the intern. The gossip flowed effortlessly throughout the office and was accepted unchallenged, owing to his well-known reputation. However, unlike most men and women whom he easily manipulated or pushed aside, this woman surprised him with a sexual harassment lawsuit that threatened his rising career. Thanks to his mentor, Jack Maloney, the lawsuit was settled relatively inexpensively, and the intern quietly moved on to another company. Schenk was pleased that he never had to apologize to the woman nor see her again, but his usual arrogant aura was diminished for an unpleasant length of time.

Similarly, the IRS case had enough holes in it that his high-priced lawyer managed to get him through with just a stern warning. He remembered having to stifle a smug smile as he stared at the lead investigator when the matter was settled. He had to content himself with enjoying the look of seething disgust on the man's face. *Just another government lackey jealous of the big boys in the private world*, he had said to himself with delicious satisfaction.

Right now, those past problems seemed laughable as he struggled to control his breathing and continued swatting those annoying biting insects away from his wounds.

"Come to India, and we'll have the adventure of a lifetime," Maloney had mentioned to him at the company

Christmas party two weeks before. Schenk remembered how Maloney smiled when he said this while gulping down some Scotch. Some of it dribbled down his chin, but he wiped it away and continued, "We're going to an important business conference in Mumbai for a few days, but we'll be spending another couple of days seeing the sights. The company wants us to build a good relationship with some of the Indian execs in the expected partnership over there, so they've given me pretty much carte blanche on the expense account. I said I needed a closer like you along, and Hammond agreed without a second thought."

"Really, Jack? I don't know shit about India," he had coolly replied. "Never been there nor ever had any interest in going there. Isn't the whole miserable place hot, crowded, and full of beggars and disease?"

"Oh, most of it truly is a cesspool," Maloney replied with a big grin, "but if you have money and know the right people, you can have an epic time. Besides, you don't have a choice, and I've never seen you turn down a chance to win some more recognition and make a nice commission. We leave Sunday, Billy Boy, so you'd better take it easy with your girl of the week. It's a long flight."

"Hey, I always did like Tandoori chicken," Schenk smirked in reply, and Maloney moved on to slobber over the CEO. "Never been with an Indian lady either, and it's on their dime," he muttered with a smug smile. He then proceeded to quickly size up the female guests at the party.

Schenk's thoughts were interrupted by the persistence of the biting insects. He weakly tried to swat them away and struggled not to lose consciousness. His mind drifted back to how well their visit to India had started.

The Indian execs had responded positively to him and

Maloney, as was normally the case. Top management admiringly called them the "dastardly dynamic duo" ("Triple D" for short) because they always got results. "Send in Triple D," was often said or written when a big contract was on the line. The Indian execs liked to talk business, but they also liked to enjoy the finer things. Schenk had gotten his Tandoori chicken and a whole lot more.

Schenk and Maloney had only glimpsed some of the impoverished neighborhoods in the city. Their driver made sure to avoid the worst areas while he whisked them to the company's headquarters and back to their luxury hotel.

Triple D's visit featured a blur of colorful restaurants accompanied by exotic music, exciting stage shows, and "private" entertainment that revealed the dream world of India to rich visitors. Schenk had been with some attractive women in his life but never with any so exotic and wild. He took full advantage of these pleasures on Maloney's expense account or on the Indian execs' bill, and he seemed even more energized than usual during their sales meetings.

Their only brief clash with some of the "cesspool" side of the country came when they first arrived at their luxury hotel, and a young boy boldly approached them. He politely but persistently claimed he had Mumbai's most beautiful handcrafted souvenirs for their consideration, but Schenk and Maloney brushed by him without a word. He kept calling after them even after they were inside the hotel. On the second day, when the boy was still pestering them and actually pulled on Schenk's Brunello Cucinelli jacket, Schenk exploded. It was one of his favorite jackets, and women loved it. He angrily pushed the boy away and brushed vigorously at the spot where he had touched the jacket. He then told the boy to get lost or else he would have him thrown in jail. The boy hung his head sadly and quietly disappeared into the bustling mob of people in the streets. Schenk then made a point to berate the front desk manager about letting "beggars" so near their luxury hotel. He ordered him to have his stylish jacket dry cleaned by that evening, or he would escalate matters. Schenk emphasized that he wanted his jacket to look perfect for that night's planned entertainment.

Schenk barked at the manager, "I can't believe I have to deal with this type of inconvenience after all the glowing reviews I've read about your hotel." His parting words were threatening and to the point as he finished his tirade saying, "Take care of things the right way or you'll soon be begging on the streets, too!"

When they were picked up the next day, the boy was nowhere to be seen. The front desk manager ushered them to their car and enthusiastically wished them a productive day. Schenk could tell his phony smile hid simmering hatred, but he gave it no further thought. The subservient manager, like all the other lowlifes in the world, was of no importance to him.

Triple D continued to work and play hard throughout their visit. During a break from one of their last meetings, Maloney laughed at a hungover Schenk and gave him a manly shove saying, "And you didn't want to come to this impoverished hellhole!"

"Change my vote to heaven on earth, Jack!" Schenk replied with a wink. "Too bad we've got to go back to reality soon."

"Hey, Billy Boy, there's one more thing I'd like to do

before we go back to our reality," Maloney said with a subdued, serious tone that surprised Schenk. "You grew up hunting, right? So did I." He now looked around to make sure nobody was in the hallway with them. "I met an interesting guy in the hotel bar last night while you were 'busy' upstairs. He says he knows someone that for a relatively reasonable price can arrange a tiger hunt for us."

Schenk recognized that Maloney knew his weaknesses—money, women, as well as hunting and other adrenaline rushes—, and he listened without interruption.

"Yeah, we both know that it's technically illegal, but we both also realize that there are always ways around things. Hell, as I've always told you, 'losers follow the rules, and winners make them!' " Maloney's face had turned even ruddier than usual, and he had a savage look in his eyes as he continued, "I've always wanted a tiger skin in my man room upstairs to be the centerpiece of my trophies. I know you can appreciate that."

Schenk had been in his impressive trophy room for many alcohol-soaked occasions, and he nodded his head steadily. He himself had also always been fascinated by the idea of bringing down something as rare, elusive, and—deadly—as a Bengal Tiger.

"My plan is to meet this contact Friday morning, and he's going to set us up with his associate who will take us to the hunting area. Supposedly, some of these tigers go off their preserves sometimes and maim and kill villagers—so we'll be practically performing a public service!" The viciousness in his face vanished as the door to the meeting room opened, and one of the Indian execs approached them. Slobbering, Christmas-party Maloney reappeared as he patted Schenk on the back and made his way toward their sales target.

That night Schenk remembered feeling more exhilarated than ever. He had hunted big game in North America but never any animal like a Bengal Tiger. He had never poached before and understood the punishment that could happen if they were caught, but this only served to make him even more excited about it. He remembered looking at that night's girl, a young beauty maybe 18, whose soft eyes betrayed her innocence. She looked terrified despite her dazzling makeup and hairstyle, which empowered him even more during their encounter. He took his prize that night with more ferocity than usual, and the woman never uttered a word of complaint. Schenk thoroughly enjoyed the feeling of her silent, trembling body underneath him.

Schenk was shocked out of his drifting recollections by a strange sound that was uncomfortably close. His hearing continued to be supernaturally good, which left him feeling even more helpless and anxious in his vulnerable position. He had also been hearing strange growls and calls that he had never heard hunting in the states. There was a crash in the brush somewhat distant, and he heard something scream out in alarm or pain. Then for a long while, there was nothing but chirping noises coming from what sounded like insects and birds. He now had picked up some other noise that made him go numb with fear.

Schenk could faintly hear something in the distance softly walking in the brush with skilled ease. He sensed its size and strength and, unmistakably, that it was stalking its prey. His pain was momentarily forgotten while he strained to hear where the animal was, and what it was doing. He tried to calm his fear by thinking of what he would do to the men responsible for all of this once he caught up with them. His mind drifted back again to the events leading up to this awful moment.

Schenk and Maloney had met the contact on Friday morning as planned. He gave them a phone number and encouraged them to take advantage of their time in India with a real adventure. Maloney called the number immediately, and they were soon picked up and driven to an exclusive hunting outfitter and then to a private airport. Within a couple of hours, they were touching down somewhere in the state of Bengal, where its namesake awaited them. Schenk noted that they were truly in a remote area with few signs of modern life. There weren't many trees, and much of the area looked like swampland surrounding a large river.

Their plan was to spend the next two days on the hunt and make it back in time for their flight home on Monday. They would buy some typical souvenirs and tell their colleagues, family, and friends about some of the great sights they saw, such as the Taj Mahal and the Agra Fort. Customs would not be a problem on either side of the trip home thanks to generous bribes. Maloney lived alone and would make up a story about inheriting the tiger skin to all but a few trusted friends.

Their lead guide, Rajiv, had met them at the airport with five other strong young men, who were outfitted for their expedition. "Mr. Maloney and Mr. Schenk, welcome to your great adventure in India!" he exclaimed with a wide grin that made them uneasy. "I trust your flight was comfortable?"

Maloney replied curtly, "Yeah, we're really looking forward to this hunt. Do you lead many of these?"

"Oh, this is something very special in my country. Consider yourself one of the privileged few to be matched with such a worthy adversary." His grin slipped for a moment and then reappeared, "I see you have already been outfitted with the proper rifles and equipment for our expedition. Excellent! We'll prepare a lunchtime feast worthy of your adventure and then set off to realize your glorious ambitions."

Schenk didn't like the flowery way Rajiv spoke or his annoying grin, but he tried not to let it bother him. He said to himself that Rajiv was just another brownnosing lackey, and that's how they talk no matter where you are in the world.

After a delicious lunch, they all climbed into the two comfortable but well-used jeeps and drove off into the swampland.

After a ride of about 90 minutes, they both started getting annoyed with Rajiv. His stories never ceased and even though they were entertaining at first, they all seemed to lead nowhere but to another story. His loud laugh and wide grin and his constant shoulder slapping were also grating on both of them. When they were at their wits' end, Rajiv shouted something to the driver and the jeeps slowly stopped.

"Lavatory break for you gentlemen," Rajiv said as he motioned to some nearby bushes in a large clearing. Neither of them had to go too badly, but they had both been grateful for the break from Rajiv and the bumpy road.

"I'm about ready to put a round into that Rajiv if he keeps up his annoying banter," Maloney joked as they both relieved themselves.

"You're not kidding! Maybe we can put him out front for tiger bait!" Schenk suggested with a snorting laugh of disgust.

"Tiger repellent is more like it, Billy Boy!" Maloney replied and they both laughed heartily.

When they turned around, they were stunned to see two of the Indian guides holding shotguns pointed at them and Rajiv and another guide searching carefully through their luggage.

His wide grin had disappeared, and he said gruffly, "Your jewelry, wallets, and passports, gentlemen."

"What the hell's going on?" Maloney barked at him. "Do you really think you can rob us like a couple of pathetic, common tourists? Our company has extensive connections in your country, you morons. They'll crush you and whatever backward crime group you work for."

"I wouldn't overestimate your importance, Mr. Maloney. Moreover, who's to say anyone will ever find out what actually happened to you. Remember how you kept all the expedition details hidden from your Indian partners and from your home company?" Rajiv smirked, patted Maloney on the shoulder, and continued, "I'm sure the authorities will think someone kidnapped you at the Taj Mahal or that you drove a jeep off the road somewhere in an attempt to go native. India is a big country, my friend, with more than a billion people, and there is always a lot going on here. What it comes down to is that you're truly insignificant, no matter how much you don't want to believe it." His wide grin appeared again at the end of his response.

Schenk remembered how he had tried to recover from his shock and negotiate his way out of their mess. It had always worked in the past, and it damned well better again.

"Rajiv, let's work something out," he began with his arms outstretched in the universal expression of no harm, no foul. "Name a price, and we'll get it for you once we're back in Mumbai. Why take the risk of getting rid of us for the small amount you'll get for our watches and wallets?" He smiled phonily and said as calmly as he could, "You bring us back to Mumbai, we'll pay you a fair sum, and we'll head back to America and never mention a word to anyone."

Of course, Schenk had tried to hide his seething anger at these peasants while he spoke. He knew that he wouldn't rest until all of them were strung up in some dark hole and tortured extensively. Despite Schenk's decades of practiced phoniness, however, Rajiv saw right through him.

"Mr. Schenk, you raise some good points, but you needn't worry about our compensation. We'll get plenty of money for your jewelry and equipment, and I'm sure your credit cards have generous credit lines that we plan to use quite promptly. Your billfolds also contain quite a bit of cash right now. In addition, your US passports will fetch a nice price in the proper circles."

Now Rajiv patted Schenk on the shoulder and continued, "Oh, I might also add that the confidential business documents you have detailing your burgeoning new partnership will be quite valuable to some of that company's competitors. Mr. Maloney's constant bragging at the bar made this abundantly clear to my colleague. No, I should say you needn't worry about our receiving enough compensation for our efforts. Believe me, sir, our risk right now is minimal compared to what it would be if we followed your scenario." He again flashed the wide grin, and now his eyes bore cruelly into both of them.

Schenk persisted even though he felt deflated, "Rajiv, I'm sure there's got to be some way—"

"Don't bother wasting your last few minutes discussing this," he interrupted. "I know your type well—disgusting, selfish, greedy leeches that have no problem exploiting anyone or anything. You do not deserve to even see an animal as majestic as the Bengal Tiger in its native habitat, let alone hunt it. Your greatest service will be to serve as food for the wild dogs and other scavengers that feed on your bloated remains." As Rajiv finished, the guide searching through the luggage yelled something to him. They all could tell from the blue stationery he held in his hand that he had found some of the confidential documents Rajiv had mentioned.

"Excuse me for a moment, gentlemen," Rajiv said with exaggerated politeness. "Why don't you make yourselves comfortable for a bit while I'm away."

The sweat that had been trickling down Maloney's face had now become a river. Schenk remembered feeling almost outside of his body as he listened to Maloney nervously whispering to him.

"We've got to make a break while we've got a chance, Bill. They don't know that I tucked a Glock in my side pocket. We can make for that grove of trees over there and follow the river until it leads us to a village or some people somewhere." He looked to make sure they weren't watching them and continued whispering, "Those bastards don't know I've also got more money stored in one of my jacket's inside pockets as well as the business card from that lowlife in Mumbai. If we can get back to civilization, we can make them all pay."

Schenk had observed the men guarding them as Maloney spoke. Only two of them held shotguns, and they were laughing and talking to each other as Rajiv and the other guide looked carefully at the confidential documents. There were also two men sitting enclosed in the other jeep listening to music and enjoying the air conditioning.

"Jack, the problem is it's at least 75 yards to those trees, and they've got us badly outgunned. You might be able to pick one or two of them off with your handgun, but the others will be after us right away. We also don't know how heavily armed the guys in the other jeep are. Maybe we should try to reason with them one more time."

"I know it's a longshot," Maloney had replied, "but it's all we've got. That Rajiv bastard made it clear that we're out of options. If I can get the two guys with the shotguns, maybe the rest of them will lose their stomach for a fight. Hell, they'll have all our valuables, and they'll think we won't be able to find the guy at the bar again."

At that point, Schenk had considered selling out Maloney. He could easily tell Rajiv about Maloney's hidden gun, the business card, and the extra cash as a gesture of good faith. However, he quickly dismissed this option when he remembered the look on Rajiv's face while he had spoken with them. That damned worm had looked upon them as scum not worthy of living. Maloney's idea was really all they had. His stomach had tightened when he fully realized that they only had one dangerous hand left to play.

Where had their plan gone wrong? Schenk thought as he lay in that godawful muck.

Those damned insects had found their second wind

and were burrowing more ferociously into his wounds. The pain was awful, but somehow he had gotten more used to it. He continued to sweat profusely and was feeling dizzy from thirst. Schenk again heard bizarre noises in the distance, but he thankfully did not hear or feel that awful stalking presence he had noticed earlier. As he looked at the small branch jammed into his leg near where the shotgun blast had torn into it, his mind returned to their escape attempt.

Maloney had nodded to Schenk as his hand slowly reached into his pocket feeling for the gun. Nobody in the group was paying them any attention because they didn't view them as a real threat. It was clear that this gang had been in this situation before and were confident how it would go. Schenk wondered how many other Western executives and tourists had found themselves in their awful shoes. Neither man said anything noteworthy nor sentimental. They liked each other, but their thoughts were only on somehow saving their own skins.

"Where had they gone wrong?" Schenk asked out loud this time.

He remembered being impressed with how smoothly Maloney had gotten the pistol out and taken aim at one of the armed guides, who was about 10 yards away. They both were going to make a break after he dropped the two guides with the shotguns. If they tried to run without taking those two out, they knew they wouldn't make it 10 feet. Schenk noticed Maloney's hand was trembling as his finger tightened on the trigger.

Everything slowed down at that point. Maloney squeezed the trigger hard, but nothing happened except for a loud click. Both men realized immediately that

Maloney had left the safety on! He quickly switched it off, but a shout arose from one of the armed guides. Maloney fired immediately, and the guide on the left screamed in pain as the bullet tore into his upper chest. Schenk remembered Rajiv looking up in shock and horror and diving behind the first jeep. Schenk himself had instinctively crouched down and was about to run. As Maloney turned to shoot the other armed guide, the man swung his barrel around and fired just before Maloney's second and third shots hit him. Schenk stared in horror as Maloney's left arm and shoulder caught the brunt of the shotgun blast, knocking him down violently. His pistol tumbled about 10 feet away from them as he fell.

Maloney stared up at him in shock and gasped in a weird high voice, "Help me up, Bill, and let's get to the damned trees!"

Schenk remembered looking back at the jeeps and seeing both armed guides down. The one on the left clearly looked dead and wasn't moving, but the one on the right was struggling to get up. His shotgun lay near him. Rajiv and the luggage-searching guide were staring at them from behind the first jeep. They were trying to tell if he and Maloney were still armed. The two guides in the other jeep had gotten out and crouched behind their doors and were also trying to see what was happening. He could not see if or how they were armed. Schenk took one last look at Maloney lying there helplessly and saw the disbelief and horror in his eyes as he began to run away.

Schenk galloped ungracefully and desperately toward the grove of trees. His years of treadmill use, pick-up basketball and weight training had helped him get to this point, but his wild running away was more reminiscent of a panicked rat.

As he ran, he heard shouts from the alarmed and angry men pursuing him. A loud shot rang out, and buckshot whistled past his head. Apparently, the other men were armed or someone (Rajiv?) had picked up one of the shotguns and fired. He glanced over his shoulder and saw at least two men after him about 30 yards back. Maloney had been right—if he could make it to the grove of trees, he would be able to hide and maybe make it down to the river and possible safety. He heard another shotgun blast, but he could tell it wasn't directed at him. *They must have finished Maloney off with that one*, he thought as his terror somehow increased.

The trees had been so painfully close that he had actually felt some hope. His thoughts about where he would hide were abruptly broken by a loud crack in the distance and a stabbing pain in his lower left side. The force of the impact violently tossed him like a rag doll to the base of the trees. He looked down and saw that a bullet had gone through his modest left love handle. He knew instantly from the sound of the weapon and the wound that someone had fired one of the high-powered hunting rifles at him. He had lain stunned for a moment, but his survival instinct had pushed him to keep crawling for some kind of cover. The land just ahead became lusher with trees and bushes as it sloped sharply down toward the riverbank. If he could somehow hide down there…

He had just started to crawl and stumble down the incline toward the river when the unmistakable boom of a shotgun went off about 20 yards behind him. This time the force shattered his right leg and some pellets ricocheted and caught him in the face. He remembered how he had tumbled completely out of control down the incline. His wild fall ended against a good-sized tree when he impaled his already-injured right leg on one of its lower branches. His already terrible pain ratcheted up to an unfathomable level. He heard excited voices and Rajiv crying out in angry triumph, and then everything had gone dark.

As he thought back on it now, he understood what had happened. After he had blacked out, the pursuing men had made it to the trees and looked down the incline toward the riverbank. They had seen his crumpled body lying about 20-30 yards down the incline among some of the thickening bushes and trees. They saw that he was covered with blood, especially his head, and decided that he was dead. None of them wanted to bother climbing down into the uninviting mixture of brush, branches, and muck where he had fallen. They were probably worried about coming in contact with poisonous snakes and other deadly animals that thrived in that habitat. Even if he had somehow survived, they knew that some creature would finish him off eventually. Maybe they had wanted it that way.

Now Schenk had managed to formulate one final plan to save himself. He was a survivor, and he would get out of this mess and have his revenge. He managed to pull the branch out of his leg and had begun the arduous task of climbing back up to level ground. His side ached, but the bleeding had stopped. His face was in agony from the shotgun pellets, but that was a secondary concern. His main worry was that his leg continued to bleed despite his fashioning of a tourniquet with his undershirt. He knew that if he continued to bleed, he would eventually lose consciousness and die. He didn't know how long he could last with his current rate of blood loss, so he worked hard to tighten up the tourniquet.

He lost track of time as he climbed up the incline. His hands slipped in the disgusting blend of mud, grass, and leaves as he inched upwards. Every now and then, he would touch something slimy that moved. He prayed that it was a frog or toad or some kind of non-poisonous snake, but who knew? The insects continued to bite him everywhere, but most painful was their attention to his open wounds. He swatted them away as best as he could, but it was hopeless.

As he stopped to rest, Schenk continued to hear strange sounds. Something yelped in the distance, and once again, he heard something moving in the brush far below him. He tried to ignore the sounds as he focused on getting to his goal: Maloney's body and hopefully his pistol.

Schenk had always had tremendous focus, which had helped him succeed in his career and with women, and he would need every bit of it now. He reasoned that if he could get to the body, he would be able to get the money out of the interior pocket. Maybe at daybreak he would be able to crawl to the beaten-up road and wait for someone to come by on foot or with a vehicle. If he was even luckier, the pistol might still be nearby. He could then shoot off some rounds to signal for help. Also, he would feel more comfortable with a weapon to guard against whatever he had heard roaming around in the brush earlier. Rajiv had also mentioned the presence of wild dogs who would happily make a meal out of him, too. Thinking of Rajiv also reminded Schenk about that business card with the first contact's name and address on it. If he could make it out alive, that card was the key to meeting up with Rajiv and his friends again. The thought of that vengeful reunion drove him the most as he slowly climbed his way up the incline.

He awoke with a start. How long had he been out? He guessed maybe an hour judging by the way the first rays of light now appeared. Dawn could not be far away. He had managed to crawl up to level ground and across most of the swampland that he had run across yesterday. That total distance of about 100 yards had taken seconds when he was running, but his crawling had lasted at least two hours. He felt lightheaded and weak, but he was still alive and determined. He even noticed that his pain had lessened a bit, and the insects had taken a break from devouring him. Maybe they didn't like the coming sunlight? Now he could clearly make out Maloney's body and lying nearby—thank God—the gun.

He wondered why they hadn't taken it with them. Maybe they were worried about the gun being traced or had just left in too much of a hurry to concern themselves with it. Farther in the distance, as the light started to shine, he noticed that there was no trace of their attackers aside from some mud tracks from their jeeps. If he could make it until daybreak and someone came along, he actually had a chance.

Schenk tried not to look at Maloney's frozen dead eyes while he fumbled through his jacket pockets. The sticky blood and oozing parts were everywhere, and he tried unsuccessfully to avoid touching them. Maloney's head had been blown nearly in a half by a shotgun blast—at least it was over quickly for him. He thought of the many alcohol-fueled adventures and business conquests he and this man had been a part of, and he shook his head slowly. "Come to India and we'll the have the adventure of a lifetime!" he said aloud while he triumphantly pulled out a wad of cash and the business card from his interior pocket. "You said it, Jack."

He struggled and crawled a bit farther to retrieve the Glock. He inspected the clip and noticed that there were 11 bullets left and one in the chamber. At least Jack had taken a couple of the bastards with him. He just wished one of them had been that scum Rajiv.

Schenk now tried to figure out his next move. His tourniquet had finally succeeded in slowing down the blood loss, but he still guessed he only had a few hours left. He would have to get lucky, or he would literally be dog meat. He decided he would wait a bit longer until it was fully light and then fire off a couple rounds to attract some locals. If he gave them enough money, maybe they could get him to a hospital or some sort of clinic.

Now he heard some movement nearby. Despite his wounds and weakened state, his hearing was still functioning at a hypersensitive level, and it had picked up something disturbing. At first, it seemed to be coming from the direction he had crawled—over near the grove of trees and the incline. Then he heard movement off to his left. Whatever it was moved quietly, but somehow he could sense its size and determination.

Schenk had the handgun in a death grip. He continued to hear the thing walking through the swampland brush. It was unmistakably stalking him, and it made him feel helpless. It was still a little too dark to make out anything clearly, but he had seen a slouching shape off to his left. With a lump in his throat, he realized that it had been following his blood trail from the trees.

Schenk made up his mind to fire a round off to see if that might scare it away, although he was afraid to waste ammunition in case it attacked. He felt he had no choice because he felt weaker with every passing minute. He pointed the gun in the general direction of where he thought he had seen the slouching shape and squeezed the trigger. There was a loud click. He couldn't believe that he had made the same mistake as Maloney—leaving the damned safety on! He quickly flicked it off, but it was too late.

At the sound of the click, Schenk saw something huge running through the swampy grass and only had a moment to bring the pistol up as it leapt upon him. He fired blindly and heard a cry of pain from his attacker. Schenk then heard a savage roar and felt the full weight of the huge animal upon him. His head and neck felt caught in an unbelievably powerful vise …

#

At midday, Sanjay decided to explore the area where he had heard all the commotion coming from in the early morning. He had finished his chores and was looking forward to some adventure to break the usual daily monotony. His father warned him to be careful because tigers and wild dogs had been seen near their village. There were also rumors going around the village of armed bandits operating in the area.

When Sanjay reached the clearing, he began to feel ill at what he saw. The man's body looked bloated in the sun, and the wild dogs had fed on him a bit. Sanjay also noticed what looked like gunshot wounds on his torso and head and that the man was unmistakably white. He seemed dressed like a hunter, but what had happened? After he steadied himself by looking away, he stifled his urge to run. Maybe there was something valuable on the man that could help his family? Just then, some scavenger birds flew off a little ways from him. Sanjay walked to where they had been eating and felt even sicker to his stomach.

The beast lay lifeless staring up at the sun, ripped apart by scavengers and something far stronger. Without another thought, Sanjay ran screaming back toward his village. As he ran, he prayed loudly for protection from the evilness of the world.

NIGHT CLOUDS

THROW IT ON THE HEAP

Lance Daniels woke up with a start after a series of disturbing stress dreams. His teeth were falling out in one, he was back in school unprepared for a test in another, and nuclear war had erupted in the worst one. The last sensation he had before jerking awake was of falling helplessly in space. His faithful cat Mortimer and loving wife Tabitha didn't stir as he leaned his ever more creaky body over the bed and headed to the bathroom. For once, it wasn't a nighttime bathroom trip out of necessity, but he thought he might as well take care of that while he was in there. The main reason for his visit was to throw some water on his face and tell himself that things were good in his life and that he shouldn't be so anxious. He was thrilled that the annual camping trip was this weekend.

Thank God for the camping trip was the mantra he concentrated on for a few precious moments of peace in the bathroom. He tried his best to avoid thinking about the many things that weighed on him:

-His crappy 9 to 5 project management job for a major corporation

-His ever-expanding waistline and thinning hair

-His hormonally challenged wife with little appetite for him but plenty for the buffet line

-His oh-so-stereotypical fanatically atheistic and parent-defying college freshman son

-His increasingly grown-up teenage daughter who he was sure was experimenting liberally with sex and drugs

and

-His eleven-year-old son who was sweet, but having a hard time paying attention in class and was starting to draw the attention of the lower forms of life that inhabit schools worldwide.

Lance's attempts to forget about these problems were futile. He rubbed his face and said, "The camping trip can't come soon enough."

The weekend started in gorgeous sunshine as he and his youngest son Charles drove toward the campsite. This unmatched fall weather was one of the reasons he stayed in New England and put up with his unsatisfying job. The light from the colorful leaves reflected playfully on his face while they made the mostly silent drive to their camping area. As was rarely the case, he had a slight smile on his face instead of his usual slight grimace.

After the usual boring camping fun with their boys on the first couple of days, the group of dads was finally at the place they most wanted to be: in front of the roaring bonfire. They had spent the day preparing for their cherished ceremony, and now it was finally time. The boys had helped out by setting up the huge bonfire during the day and were allowed to roast marshmallows and hot dogs while it was still in its infancy. The youngsters were all safely sleeping in their tents at this late hour. Now this crackling treasure of heat and energy and huge dancing flames was all for the fathers.

Lance's neighbor, Jay, stood up, tapped his beer can in exaggerated ceremonial fashion with a plastic Spork, and proclaimed in his funny fake British accent, "We are all duly assembled here in the year of our Lord 2017 to let our voices be heard in the heavens. Keep calm and carry on, and tally ho! God Save the Queen, Monday Night Football, and Clint Eastwood. Let the majestic ceremony of the fire and the heap begin!"

Jay then continued, "As this year's appointed master of ceremonies, I have the honor of the first offerings to the fire and to the heap."

A cheer erupted from the group of men watching from their lawn chairs that ringed the fire.

"My first offering is to the fire. This is a photo of my dear boss, who I think might be somehow related to Hitler or maybe some South American dictator. This sorry excuse for a human being managed to yell at me in front of the whole office for not meeting my sales goals, steal my best ideas and claim credit for them, and spread rumors behind my back. He then surpassed all that treachery by not laying me off in the most recent round but still finding a way to stick me with twice as much work and a 20% salary reduction. With all that bad behavior, I say that we throw this evil creature into the fire!"

The group's cry began softly at first, and then it rose into a loud rhythmic chant: "Throw him into the fire! Throw him into the fire! Throw him into the fire! Throw him into the fire!"

Jay slowly encouraged the chanting until it reached an almost deafening level, and then with a few contrived dance moves for effect, he tossed the photo into the fire. It was consumed in an instant, and the crowd cheered its approval.

After the furor died down, Jay began the next part of the ritual. "My offering for the heap concerns my lovely ex-wife." He pulled out a Mercedes hood ornament and cradled it in his hand.

"This is from my dream car that I worked my ass off for, which she, of course, got in our unfair divorce settlement. Her lawyer was far sleazier than mine and managed to spread enough rumors and innuendo about me that I didn't stand a chance." He paused and slowly turned the ornament around a couple of times in his hand then continued, "My wife didn't even care that much about the car when we were together, but she knew she could hurt me by taking it away. I went by the other day and 'borrowed' this part from it, just to try and remember what it was like driving it … at least for a little while." His voice caught a bit at the end, and you could see some redness in his eyes despite his drunken grin.

"I've had it long enough now, so I think it's time I throw it on the heap!"

The crowd roared its approval.

Jay walked behind the fire with the others following him in a primitive dance line chanting: "Throw it on the heap! Throw it on the heap! Throw it on the heap!"

He went only a short distance and stood at the top of a huge pit they had dug a few years earlier when the tradition began. Other heap items, most damaged in some way, filled the bottom of the pit: home appliances, jewelry, computers, phones, old camcorders. One of the largest and most surprising items was an electric golf cart. Getting that into the pit was a story in itself.

As the chanting continued, Jay hurled the ornament into the center of the heap. It skittered around a bit and settled next to a dented monogrammed flask that had been a best man's gift when life was full of hope and vitality.

John, the sole bachelor in the group and Lance's closest friend in the neighborhood, was next.

"This is a postcard I got from my friend, Simon, who was recently visiting Machu Picchu and observing endangered birds in Peru with his latest environmentally conscious twenty-something girlfriend. It has this simple message on it: *Living the Dream, dude! Keep freezing your ass off in New England!*"

He looked down for a moment then continued, "This guy, who is a dear friend in many ways, has been married twice, doesn't have time for his kids, and has been dating a slew of good-looking young women for the last couple of years. I should also mention that he made a fortune selling his company that provides herbal remedies for stress (none ever scientifically proven of course), and now he doesn't work at all."

John, who had been set to marry the love of his life before she rejected him out of a desire to "explore my inner self first," had never gotten around to finding someone new to marry. He was also an aspiring musician who wrote and played great music, but he would never make enough money to go to Peru to observe rare birds.
He said with a quivering voice, "I think you can understand why I am offering this postcard to the fire."

The crowd was a bit muted at first, and then an even

rowdier chanting ceremony than Jay's ensued. The bonfire hungrily consumed the postcard as the group cheered wildly.

"My offer for the heap is pretty basic, and one that we can all appreciate," John continued. "I just can't take any more social media. The constant messages, tweets, selfies, hashtags, and annoying videos are just sapping my soul. I hereby offer my tablet to the heap." The crowd started cheering, but he hushed them with raised arms and declared, "I would also like to use 'the Royal Sledgehammer!' "

The men cheered even louder and began the chant of "Throw it on the heap!" Then someone in the group used their phone to play a music video of "Sledgehammer," by Peter Gabriel. Delirium reigned as John raised the sledgehammer and smashed the tablet into multiple small pieces. He picked up as many pieces as he could find and threw them on the heap.

When it was Lance's turn, he produced a business envelope saying, "This is the rejection letter I got when I applied for a small business loan to start my paint-it-yourself art gallery business. The bank said I was just too overextended with all my family's expenses, and I didn't have sufficient collateral. They didn't believe in the viability of my business idea either." He paused for a second, and the only sound was the loud crackling of the bonfire.

"Just a few weeks ago, however, I noticed that the mayor's wife leased out the spot I was planning on using and is starting up a very similar business there." He looked around at the others, and they shook their heads in solidarity. He continued, "Funny thing is, we all know how tight the bank's owner is with the mayor and that their wives head the civic league together. For their stinginess and central role in hindering my life's dream, I hereby offer the bank's rejection letter to the fire. May its noxious fumes linger over and poison that damned bank and business forever!" The men cheered and danced maniacally when Lance threw the envelope and its depressing contents into the raging bonfire.

When things had died down again, Lance spoke softly, "My offer for the heap is this worthless piece of plastic they call a health insurance card. It doesn't insure my family or me too well, even when the premium is sky high, and the deductibles keep getting higher. There's almost nothing it pays for short of an extended hospital stay or a major procedure. I'm paying out of pocket for everything else despite the high premium." His face now was filled with anger as he continued, "For its role in taking more and more of my precious resources and giving less and less in return, I hereby offer this health insurance card and the despicable company and business model it represents to the heap. May they please go bankrupt before our next ceremony!"

With that final declaration, Lance took out his fishing knife and angrily gouged out a series of different-sized holes in the insurance card. He then threw the mutilated card into the middle of the heap. The men roared their approval and danced with him as he tossed the card on the heap. They then all made a couple of frenzied conga line loops around the fire, laughing and yelling the entire time.

After everyone who wanted to had taken their turn, and the fire and the heap had been fed with some of life's miseries, it was now time for the speed round.

During this part of the ceremony, a notebook was passed around, and the participants could write down and call out other annoying things they wanted to denigrate and destroy.

Some old favorites were enthusiastically yelled out or written down:

Lying politicians
Greedy lawyers
Political correctness
Religious fanatics
Pop culture
Boy bands
College tuition
Vet bills
Taxes
Arrogant, overpaid, disloyal athletes
US military involvement
Race baiters and poverty pimps
Government shutdowns
Social justice warriors
Virtue signaling
The Fed
The UN
Arms dealers
Bank fees
White guilt
Corporate cronyism
White-collar criminals
Paparazzi
Reality celebrities
Fraudulent science

Climate change
Climate change deniers
Investment bankers
Political consultants
Pollsters
Hypocritical protesters
Self-righteous people
So-called elites
Phony outrage
Warmongers
Contractors
Infomercials
Agents and Commissions
Predatory towing
Limousine liberals
Rednecks
Thursday Night Football
Out of touch academics
Holy rollers
Atheist fanatics
The Media
Fake news
Political parties
Gun nuts
Convenience fees
Pyramid schemes
Low-fat diets
Speed cameras
Award shows

In addition, a few random ones appeared:

Celebrities with too much plastic surgery
Car insurance commercials
Sequels
Talking clowns
Organic pizza
White rappers
Smartphone addicts
Outdoor weather reporters in treacherous conditions
Jazzercise
Hyphenated last names
Laundry detergent pod challenges
Food selfies

As was the tradition, Jay tore out the notebook's paper sheets with the cursed terms and tossed them into the bonfire. He then took the rest of the notebook, which had *2017* written on its cover in bright red ink, and threw it on the heap.

The noise died down, and the beautiful cathartic moment was over. Jay closed the session with mock formality, and then everyone kept drinking and exchanging jokes and light-hearted stories for a couple hours. At about 4 AM, a few of the more sober dads doused the slowly diminishing bonfire with some buckets of water from the nearby pond.

The first boys woke up around 9 AM and roused the dads for the traditional morning swim and flapjack brunch. Then they were all on their way back home for another year in their interesting lives.

On the drive home, Lance wondered how the Pats would do on Monday Night Football tomorrow as Brady wasn't getting any younger.

THE TRAMPS

Both astronauts knew they were in trouble even before the first warning signals started to obnoxiously beep and blink. Captain Lawrence Malburne and First Lieutenant Peter Lipmann were experienced pilots who knew the art and science of space flight well.

They had both immediately noticed the way their huge cargo vessel had started to fly sluggishly after passing through a strange dark cloud of an unknown, gaseous material. Neither of them had ever experienced anything like it. It reminded Lipmann of the ominous way the sky looked over the Great Plains in a tornado disaster movie he had seen a few years back. Both men were especially annoyed that their flight computer could not provide them with any relevant analysis of the anomaly.

Captain Malburne had been a squadron leader for a few years flying single engine fighters during the Pluto Mining War of the last decade. Lieutenant Lipmann had been a transport ship commander during that same conflict. Since the war had ended decisively a few years back, United Flight Command didn't have nearly as much use for pilots, and they had given about 80% of them their notice. Neither Malburne nor Lipmann had complained too much because they both received honorable discharges and decent pensions. They both also had plenty of contacts in the booming world of commercial cargo transport and knew they would easily be able to secure steady work. They were also well aware that the new job would be boring and predictable compared to the adrenaline-filled military campaigns they had experienced, but no civilian position could compare with that wild rush.

Malburne and Lipmann had been the pilot and co-pilot of the massive C-Class Cargo Vessel called *Quintus* for the last three years. They had been matched up as a flight crew for their psychological compatibility, determined after many rounds of personality testing. Compatibility was definitely of the utmost importance when you were making the four-month roundtrip from Pluto's Vanguard Station to resupply the mining outpost on faraway Omega Seven. Their employer, Prism Transport, was the leading supply transporter in the system, and they didn't take any unnecessary risks with their lucrative cargo.

The men's contracts with Prism also stipulated that they were not allowed to be married, have significant others, or father any children during their service time. Prism was also right to have those conditions considering the type of jobs they offered. The company definitely knew what they were doing when it came to making certain their long-range transports ran smoothly.

The two astronauts had quickly confirmed the effectiveness of Prism Transport's patented compatibility testing. The men had bonded immediately and had become fast friends during their five previous round-trip missions. They also had never so much as had a minor equipment malfunction or course correction during those missions. Their flight computer and the skill and efficiency of the pilots had ensured that result. However, none of that stellar compatibility, training, experience, or unblemished flight history seemed to matter now; all because of, as Lipmann crudely described it, "some bullshit dark cloud made up of who the fuck knew what."

After hitting the destructive cloud, the pilots' training in emergency situations immediately booted up, and they began their respective checklists. Unfortunately, the usual emergency procedures weren't working well because most of their flight systems were not responding normally. The most important tool to help them, the flight computer, remained silent while they tried desperately to assess their worsening situation.

"I've got major system malfunctions in navigation and communications, and more importantly, in life support and propulsion," Lipmann reported with clenched teeth.

"Ok, Lip, let's determine if this baby can be saved or not, so tell me what is working," Malburne replied with concern and a strong emphasis on "is." He struggled to restart the flight computer and then switched to manual controls to try to get them back on course. The *Quintus* continued its sluggish roll to nowhere.

After about 10 long seconds, Lipmann reported, "I'm sorry, Cap. I can't get a reading on anything functioning anywhere near normal, and backup systems are dead. Even worse, it looks like the core shielding system is permanently down, which gives us about 30 minutes before the propulsion system blows."

"Lip, you're just full of cheery news," Malburne replied with a frown. He then coolly continued, "Let's plan a First Emergency EVAC. Use the manual charts to see what's in range of the life star."

"Roger that, captain … ah just give me a second to do it the old-fashioned way," Lipmann replied as he pulled out the relevant charts from underneath the guidance system. After about 30 seconds, which seemed much longer to both of them, he finally answered, "It looks like Asteroid XUM-1609 is the only solid object within range of the life star. We'll have to wait it out on that big ugly rock until the cavalry comes looking for us."

"Let's initiate emergency evacuation procedures and salvage whatever we can from her."

Lipmann began the procedures, but most of the steps involved sending distress signals with their various communications systems. Unfortunately, none of them were working, so they skipped down the protocol list. Most importantly, the men rummaged through the *Quintus'* galley and transferred as much food and water as they could carry into the life star escape vessel. Lipmann also took the portable entertainment system from his quarters hoping that it would still be functional with its durable, self-charging batteries.

As their last official action on the *Quintus*, both men wrote down brief entries in the rarely used official logbook hard copy. They both described the strange anomaly that forced their evacuation. They also noted the date and time of evacuation and the location of the asteroid where they would be awaiting rescue. After their quick summaries were completed, they placed the logbook in a fire retardant bag and sealed it in a protected small chamber under the guidance system. The men both hoped that their rescue would come from someone who never laid eyes on this logbook. They understood that it would probably be months or even years before anyone discovered the remnants of their lost ship in this remote sector.

Warning messages now blared, *Propulsion System critically exposed! Recommend immediate evacuation of all crewmembers. Ten minutes until critical mass is reached!* The message repeated loudly as the two entered the life star and closed its hatch.

"Well, at least this hunk of junk has some functionality," Malburne said with faint hope in his voice while he examined the controls of their new vessel.

"As long as we can get out of here and make it to that rock, we've at least got a chance, right?" Lipmann said with his own brief bit of optimism. "C'mon you bastard, give me a little something to hang onto, alright?"

"Sure, Lip," Malburne replied with a tight grin. "Don't you know that assholes like us always make it in the end!"

The life star's manual controls responded, and Malburne was able to successfully detach the vessel and start the journey to the asteroid. Lipmann reported on the craft's status, "Life support systems and manual navigation functioning normally. Emergency beacons and most communications systems malfunctioning."

Before Malburne could reply to this report, there was a bright flash from an explosion that they both knew signaled the end of the *Quintus* as a working spaceship. Lipmann looked through one of the viewing windows and said, "That girl served us well during our time with Prism. Now she's just some burned out sections of space junk. Farewell, baby."

"Goodbye, old girl," was all Malburne could muster as he tried to orient himself with the unfamiliar controls of the life star.

"She was really a boring shit bucket, but she was our shit bucket. She was our home and got the job done for quite a while, Cap," Lipmann added as he watched the remnants of the ship float away. He closed his eyes for a second, tried not to panic, and then went back to his calculations.

"Well, Captain Malburne," Lipmann said a short time later, "using old-fashioned navigation skills my professors back at the academy would be proud of, I've figured out our course to that rock and about how long it will take to get there."

"Ok, Lip, your new title is Navigator Extraordinaire. Let me hear the good news, your majesty."

"It's going to take us about three days, and we're going to need some serious piloting skills to land on it without any help from a flight computer. But, if we do make it down there, we should be able to last 4-6 weeks with our supplies and the life support systems—as long as we ration things out carefully."

"Nothing left to do now, but plot the course and get to our new home rock. Let's hope it's a short visit!" Malburne said to his close friend with a reassuring pat on the back.

#

Lipmann's calculations were correct, and three days later they were orbiting the large asteroid that they hoped would be their temporary sanctuary. Their readings indicated that its size and its heavy concentration of iron and nickel would give it just a little less than Earth standard gravity on the surface.

Both men were extremely skilled pilots, and they managed to expertly guide the vessel down to what looked like a relatively level landing site. They noted that there were some huge rock outcroppings and massive canyons nearby, so they took special care to not lose their concentration during the landing. The manual controls were difficult to operate, but they managed to get the life star down with a rough, but safe landing.

"Honey, we're home! Where's my dinner?" Lipmann exclaimed as they touched down. Malburne laughed with relief as Lipmann continued, "Nice job, Cap. That probably topped any piloting you had to do during the war."

"Thanks, Lip. Everything is a little bit easier when you don't have pricks shooting at you!"

Over the next few days, the men made the life star as comfortable as they could and organized a rationing system that would enable them to live for as long as possible while awaiting rescue. Their main problem was the amount of water available. Their life support system would easily last a few months. They had plenty of food, but they only had a thirty-day supply of water in the life star, and there wasn't a drop of it on their new cold and dark home. They both knew that they could only last a few days without it.

"Hey, Burnsy!" Lipmann called over to Malburne, switching to the nickname he used when they were off duty. He knew they weren't going to be flying an official mission for a while. "Here's the good news. I've managed to get the communications system to work but only at a limited range. I'll keep sending out the standard SOS alerts and hope we get lucky. Someone's got to come by this miserable big space boulder at some point, right?" He waited for Malburne's head nod and continued, "Also, after not receiving our daily status check-in, Prism will have launched a rescue mission to our last known position. Something's got to break our way, don't ya think? Oh, and there's some other good news. My battery-powered entertainment system was damaged in the landing, but it will still play one song."

"Just one? Well, I guess it's better than nothing. It better be a good one!"

"It was in the *Old American Crooning Classics* folder, from a famous singer named Frank Sinatra. The song is called 'The Lady is a Tramp.' "

"Frank Sinatra?" Malburne repeated with a quizzical expression. "Oh yeah!" As a smile crossed his face he continued, "I remember my grandfather talking about him some. He was well before his time, too, but he said Sinatra was a legendary singer in the 20th Century with a ton of popular songs. I think he was supposed to also be about as cool as you can get and loved equally by the ladies and guys." He closed his eyes and concentrated saying, "I remember listening to a few songs by him when I was a kid. There was a catchy one about New York that I recall because it really made me want to visit a city that never went to bed or something like that. I wasn't sure what that meant, but it sounded exciting to me. I also remember seeing Sinatra on some old documentaries performing and holding court with other celebrities … but I never heard of that 'tramp' song you just mentioned."

"Well, Burnsy, you're going to get to know it well, believe me. Unless I can somehow improve my tinkering skills dramatically during our stay, that's the only damned song I can get this thing to play!"

#

Their one source of entertainment played with great clarity inside the cramped confines of the life star. They listened to the song again in silence. They had heard it many times by now, but neither man had grown tired of it. The words were somewhat exotic and old-fashioned—something about a lady enjoying the theater and not hanging around with people she didn't like. Malburne finally broke the silence saying, "What I can't figure out is if being a 'tramp' is a good thing or not. Nobody has used that word in a long time, huh? I thought it meant a woman with, shall we say, loose moral virtues."

Lipmann eagerly replied, "No, no, no! It does mean something like that, but you're missing the point of the song. He's saying that the other women insult her because they don't like how she doesn't fall in line with the rest of them. Nobody likes a non-conformist, and that goes for any era."

"I don't know, Lip. It still seems a little insulting, but I guess he's trying to make a point."

"Exactly."

The song kept playing with Sinatra's powerful voice enunciating every syllable. Now he was singing about the lady not playing some sort of games and visiting Harlem without wearing something called 'ermine.' Then there was a line about her not gossiping with other women.

"You see! You get it now, Burnsy?" Lipmann asked. "She's not a phony like so many others. This lady is not petty and not afraid to be herself. She does what she wants and has her own opinions about things! That's why she gets badmouthed, but it's also why she's so attractive to some people."

"A real rebel, huh? I guess there's something alluring about people like that in any era, huh?"

"You said it, my friend! Consider how life was for women back in the 20th Century. I think they had just recently gotten the right to vote and manually drive vehicles. I don't think many of them had any real career opportunities either. A total joke really, when you think about it."

"Wow! Unbelievable stuff. You do know your history and are a damn fine song analyst, Lip. But now for the real test … What the hell is 'ermine?' "

Lipmann started to mumble something, but Malburne cut him off with a big laugh and clapped him on the shoulder. "You see, mister expert analyst, some eternal mysteries do remain!" Both men laughed loudly.

A few days later, the men were listening intently to their main source of entertainment again. They were trying hard to understand the strange lyrics, which again centered on some type of gambling in a place called Harlem.

Lipmann piped up to break the repetition of the song, "I still can't figure some of these lyrics out. I know 'crap games' are some kind of gambling, but I can't really picture them. Can you? Not sure what the hell a 'sharpie' is, but a 'fraud' seems clear. What I don't understand is why everyone wants her to go to Harlem." He closed his eyes and thought for a second then continued, "I think it was some trendy, rich neighborhood in New York City or Boston, but I'm not sure. I've only been to Earth once and nowhere close to those cities."

Malburne answered, "From what my grandmother used to say, a lot of us darker people lived in their own distinct areas like that, back when the races didn't mix as much. I think Harlem was one of the most famous black neighborhoods. I know it produced a lot of great literature and music, especially in the 20th Century around Sinatra's time.

"So, who's the historian now, ay Burnsy?" Lipmann asked with a grin. "Maybe we should start teaching each other about the most interesting things we learned in school and from our elders. That will help pass the time until we're rescued, right?"

"Why not, Lip? We sure don't need to learn anything new about piloting, warfare, science, or other practical stuff at this point." He leaned back, and his stretched out legs bumped into Lipmann in their cramped quarters. He nodded his head and continued, "It would be nice to learn some things just to know them, you know what I mean? Things like history, art, and, of course, music. You're up first, buddy."

"I'll tell you one thing. I'd take a few hours or even minutes with any lady right about now, and we could discuss any of those topics. And I don't care about any of their 'virtues.' I'd just like to hear their sweet voice and feel comforted by a softer presence." He looked out the window of the life star at the asteroid's dark, bleak, rocky terrain and frowned. "No offense, Burnsy, but you're getting kinda scary to look at and talk to lately. That beard is really an eyesore, my friend. I might even donate today's water ration and help you shave off that monstrosity!"

'Don't get any fresh ideas, Lip. Take it easy, now, because we don't have enough water to hose you down!"

They both laughed for a little while and then were silent again for at least ten minutes while the song played again.

Malburne finally broke their silence saying, "I really like this song and how he sings, but I wish we had that New York one, too. Damn! I really enjoyed hearing it back when I was a kid."

"Maybe the next time we're marooned on a lifeless asteroid in the dark void of space, we'll make a point to arrange to have that one for you instead, Burnsy!"

Both men laughed again for a long time.

A couple of weeks had passed in the life star, and the men had developed a boring routine that involved frequent attempts at distress calls with their limited communications system, regular meals with strict water consumption, and finding ways to pass the time.

They carefully rationed the water and splurged some on the food, as they had plenty of that. They were resourceful enough to fashion a metal strainer with a filter, which made their urine drinkable, and they preserved every drop of juice from the fruit containers. They also avoided any salty food to lessen their desire for water as much as possible. Even still, they were soon constantly thirsty and getting more lethargic.

One day, to raise their spirits and break the crushing monotony, Malburne suggested they take a stroll around their surroundings and get some exercise. They were both psychologically certified to handle being in cramped quarters for lengthy trips, but they were being severely tested by the life star's small dimensions. They suited up and walked out to the huge canyon they had observed during their landing. It was a little more than two kilometers from the life star. The men managed to get there in less than an hour by alternately walking and hopping in the slightly reduced gravity. They made sure to proceed at a leisurely pace because the last thing they needed was to sweat and consume more water.

When they got near the edge, both men gasped in astonishment at the width and depth of the massive canyon. The bright colors of the rocks and the endless variety of formations were beautiful and intimidating at the same time. They had to adjust their helmet visors to reduce the reflected brightness.

"That's the biggest and most beautiful canyon I've ever seen, Burnsy," Lipmann said. "I think it probably has the Grand Canyon, Valles Icarus, and Valles Marineris beat! You ever see anything like that?"

"Nope. I can't even see the bottom of it from here. It must go many kilometers down. Don't get too close to the edge. The gravity on this big rock is a little less than Earth standard, but not enough to stop a long fall to infinity."

"When we get back, I've got dibs on arranging tourist trips to that canyon. If you're interested, we could make a fortune!"

Malburne responded with a thumbs up, and they started back to the life star.

A few days after their outing, Lipmann seriously began thinking about killing Malburne. If he did it, he knew he would immediately double his remaining possible lifespan. His cold, simple calculation was that gaining that precious additional time would mean a decent increase in his chance of being rescued. He even rationalized that it would be doing his friend a favor. It was clear to him that Malburne was suffering under these conditions even more than he was.

The act itself wouldn't be easy for him, but he rationalized that it would be a mercy killing. It was getting hard to focus his thoughts, but he went over this option repeatedly in his head and came up with a plan. First, he would knock Malburne unconscious after he had fallen asleep. Then he would use some of their thick repair tape to block his airways, and that would be that. It would be quick and painless—a blessing really when you thought about it.

After considering his plan for a few days, Lipmann decided it wasn't worth it. How would he live with himself even if he were eventually rescued? The awesome guilt from killing his good friend would surely end his life not long after getting off this stinking rock.

Something in his friend's eyes told him that Malburne had already considered this disturbing option, too. Prism really was spot on about their compatible mindsets.

He decided not to worry about any possible attack from his friend, as he was confident that Malburne had reached the same conclusion. Even if he hadn't, Lipmann was reasonably sure he wouldn't feel a thing anyway.

Over the next couple of weeks in the life star, the men talked occasionally and listened to their one song. The jokes weren't coming like before. Time passed and grim reality firmly began to take hold. Frank, however, continued to sing with his usual vim and vigor: Now he was singing about how the lady liked to feel the wind in her hair, but she was "broke" somehow. She also hated California's weather, which was strange to them because they had always heard it was pleasant there.

The ancient song was still confusing to the men, but they felt they had made progress in understanding a decent amount of it over the course of their stay. Their many conversations about the song's meaning and about society back in the 20th Century had sure helped pass the time during their unwanted stay.

Finally, Lipmann broke their silence. They both were talking in croaking voices now, but they were determined to keep their conversations going. Even though it hurt like hell to talk, it was worth it to divert their thoughts from their situation.

"Hey, you know, that's it! I think a tramp also used to mean someone without money, someone broken or 'broke,' traveling around out in the wilderness without much means to support themselves…" His words were interrupted abruptly by an intense and awful hacking cough—something that had started to happen more frequently with both of them. He tried to spit out whatever he had hacked up, but barely a drop of liquid came out of his dried-up mouth. He softly rubbed his throat and continued in his raspy voice, "I think a lot of those tramps rode on trains and hitched rides heading who knows where. You know something, they didn't have money or security, but they had their freedom. Sounds kinda romantic and adventurous, doesn't it?"

"A little, Lip. Most of them probably died in remote places without anyone knowing or caring," Malburne answered in a wistful and defeated tone that disturbed Lipmann.

"Sounds familiar, doesn't it, Burnsy?" Lipmann said to his friend with a hopeful smile trying to cheer him up a bit.

"I'd like to think some people care about us, but I get your point."

"Look at it this way, my friend. I bet nobody has ever

tramped to this ugly rock before. Hey, and I know nobody has ever listened to Mr. Frank Sinatra crooning on it, that's for sure!"

Malburne's head shot back as he roared with laughter that no cough could stop. "That's definitely gotta count for something, Lip!"

The men both laughed for a long time and hugged.

A few days after the water had run out, the men were back at the edge of the giant canyon. They were both incredibly weak, so it had taken them a good while to get there. Their journey was more of an awkward shuffle than a hike as they held each other up the whole way. The men had written down what they needed to in the life star. Lipmann had brought along their beloved entertainment system and played their song one more time.

They listened to the song play once through without any commentary. Sometime after it started playing again, Lipmann tossed the little entertainment system high up in the air, and it plummeted out of sight heading toward the bottom of the canyon. It didn't fall as fast as it would on Earth, but it fell fast enough. Sinatra's powerful voice projected defiantly as it dropped, emphasizing that the lady sure was a tramp.

The song echoed off the massive canyon walls and lingered for a surprising amount of time in the hostile atmosphere, but then silence reigned. The words and music were long since imprinted in their minds.

Lipmann broke the silence with his raspy voice saying, "You know what's funny? I already miss hearing that song. Who would've thought that, huh?"

"Me, too," Malburne said with a smile. "Thanks for everything, Frank." After about a minute, Malburne turned to his good friend and said, "I guess it's about time, Lip."

"Yep. It sure is, Burnsy. We had a hell of a run, but it's time for the tramps to go home."

There was nothing left to say at that point, as they had discussed everything of importance and everything not of importance many times over. There was not enough moisture left in either of them for any tears.

They looked each other square in the eyes, hugged briefly, joined hands, and jumped into the abyss.

NIGHT CLOUDS

SEB'S ROCK

September 22, 1831

It don't look like much now, that wagon sized rock ledge settin' by itself in the middle of that field. Folks around here call it Patriots Ledge or some other glorious names, but it'll always just be Seb's Rock to me.

There's an impressive memorial plaque there they put up maybe ten years after the war and some people place little flags, flowers, and ribbons in the ground near it sometimes. You can also always count on some group of old soldiers to celebrate it once in a while with grand toasts, music, and speeches. I myself don't like going out that way. I don't get much peace from it, even though it's been more than fifty damned years now since it all happened. If it were up to me, I would have moved away long ago from this place, but my missus still had a lot of family settled here, so that was the end of that notion.

This pretty famous fella from the newspaper down Hartford way wants to do a story on what happened in some of the local battles around here during our glorious War of Independence. I guess it's to celebrate the 50th anniversary of our victory at Yorktown, which pretty well put things to rest.

I don't know who sent him to me—maybe Ned Samuels or one of the few other relics like me still above ground that fought way back then. Ned didn't really see much action, but he sure has always liked to prattle on. Most of us that did see our share of fighting don't talk much about it. I've refused to talk to anyone official about it fer so long, and I was going to respectfully decline again, but my wife pleaded with me to just go on and get it all out once and fer all. She said that maybe then I can meet my maker in peace and possibly end those occasional night terrors. Those beauties don't happen that often, but when they do, boy—it really is like gettin' a visit from some nasty little demons from hell.

I'll go ahead then and do it to make her happy, but I know it ain't never gonna stop those demons from coming fer me some nights when they really want to pay me their respects. I'll also do it even more fer Seb though, 'cuz I was real fond of that boy, and maybe it will help keep his memory alive in people's minds a bit longer anyway. Rightly so. Better the attention be on his memory instead of those pompous windbags whom we have to listen to whenever the subject of our war comes around.

I hope at least he could stay in people's minds until the next big war anyway—and we all know that's just a matter of time—when the whole lot of us will be well forgotten.

I thought about telling this journalist fella what

happened face to face like he requested, but I don't want to be interrogated about the little details like some common thief. That's why I've decided to put everything that's relevant all down in this here letter that I'll send to him along with another copy to a local library company. They can all then do with it what they want. I won't be around much longer to protest or care in any case. Maybe writing everything down will help keep those night basterds away fer some of the little time I got left anyway.

Sebastian Fenton was the boy's full name. I'm not sure how old he was when he came to us, but I'd be surprised if he had yet reached a full 16 years. He was as thin as a scarecrow and pale skinned with thick, wavy brown hair. You could tell his frame warn't near filled out and he had some decent growing left in him. At first, some of us thought he came to serve as a drummer boy, but that warn't the case. No sir. From afar he looked like an innocent child in need of protection, but the way he spoke and carried himself would have better fit a much older fella.

When we first saw him, we started teasin' him, like we did with all the fresh fish—but it never did feel right with Seb. We would say leading things and make jokes to get a rise out of him like with the other greenhorns. Seb there, however, would always just keep that same calm expression with his dark brown eyes firmly fixed upon you and would never take the bait. I never once saw him get angry or the least bit visibly bothered. He reminded me of an eager to please, but calm old dog or something, but lemme tell you he also had a powerful brain in that young head of his. Pretty soon we all knocked off the teasing 'cuz it just didn't fit and made us uncomfortable.

Some guys had started off calling him Sebastian or Fenton, but he would always answer calmly that we should just call him Seb like his pappy done, so that's what we did. Nobody ever called him kid because it just didn't fit neither.

I'll tell ya, Seb's nose was always in a book when he warn't on duty. He used to like to quote interesting lines from the many books he read that were always comforting and sometimes amusing. Some of the lines were from Shakespeare and other famous writers, and some were from books and authors I couldn't even rightly pronounce. He also knew the good book inside and out.

Seb would always seem to offer us a line of wisdom that somehow fit our current miserable situation. One he used a lot was "Cry 'havoc' and let slip the dogs of war." When someone complained about the freezing cold he would say, "Now is the winter of our discontent," and then he'd kick the snow on the ground in mock disgust. If someone bleated about some thankless task, he would always say to them, "I prefer to do right and get no thanks than to do wrong and receive no punishment." Another line he frequently said was, "The greatest among you will be your servant."

My favorite line though was one I only heard him say the last time I spoke to him when I inquired if he were scared about the upcoming battle. He smiled and said, "Cowards die many times before their deaths; the valiant never taste of death but once."

There were many others, but those few I still remember clear as day. I'm not sure where those beautiful wise sayings came from, but they always seemed to calm people down and bring smiles when we sure needed them. We all loved him fer that.

I should probably add here that Seb also helped me and others improve our writing and reading abilities. Any poor grammar or spelling in this letter is on my account not his.

Another peculiar thing about Seb we noticed was he used a pair of brass spectacles to help him read sometimes. It was odd, but his vision was already going at such a young age. Those spectacles made him even more unusual and endeared him to us all even more. He hid them in the pocket of his coat when he warn't using them.

What caught the colonel's attention was when Seb mentioned how his dad had larned him in the use of whale oil. They had used it to not only light up their home with lanterns but to somehow help clear their fields outside of Danbury. I think his pappy had been on a whaling ship fer a good spell out of New Bedford afore he moved to Danbury and he knew a lot about whales and their precious oil. Not sure how his dad came to all his knowledge or could afford those luxuries, but Seb larned his lessons well. None of us farm boys had ever been to sea, so those things were all a mystery to us.

Just a bit of background about me and the rest of the boys. We had inlisted enthusiastically right near the beginning of the affair. Our local outfit saw a lot of action in New York and New Jersey afore returning back home to Connecticut in desperate shape.

Listening to people talk now, you'd think winning our independence was as sure as another freezing cold winter up here, but it warn't nowhere near such a thing. The Redcoats and their German mercenaries, known as the Hessians, were beating the tar out of us fairly good fer the first couple of years. Things were goin' so awful that a decent amount of fellas in our forces didn't stay when their inlistment expired or just plain deserted. It's hard to blame them boys too much as we barely ever got paid and seemed to be starving, freezing, or both a good deal of the time I can tell ya. With things looking bad, a good chunk of the local people throughout the colonies either went Tory or did nuthin' to help our patriotic cause. Believe me, ya don't hear that dark history talked about much anymore, but I lived through it.

Seb joined us in the time when we were in bad shape in Connecticut. He never really saw much action, as we were only involved in some minor skirmishes, spendin' most of our time and energy retreating from the Crown's superior forces. I don't think I ever saw him unshoulder and fire his musket—he had enough trouble just carrying the thing.

During that time, Seb sure did suffer with us in our desperate marching all around the area. He was mighty weak by the time we reached that last cow pasture with the rock. He also got to live in the filth of our various encampments and eat our sorry scraps of food, which made him even thinner. And, I tell ya, he never complained a single time about none of it. As I already mentioned, he spent his time and energy cheering others up no matter how weak he seemed.

I myself was a farm boy who hadn't traveled much, so everything in the war was new to me including this here little town where the battle happened. We had fought the Redcoats to a stalemate outside Danbury, and our unit had drawn up our defensive line right at the edge of that big cow pasture. There was a wagon sized rock ledge right in the middle of it, maybe left by one of them big icebergs thousands of years ago, as some folks tell it. The colonel knew the enemy would have to march right through the main road and fields on their way to Norwalk and other destinations of military importance (I think we had some powder houses and weapons stored in various locations that they were interested in, but the details escape me now.). We always seemed just one more thrashing away from losing the whole damned thing, I can tell ya that, but the higher ups were sweating even more than usual on this here occasion.

Our spies and scouts told us we didn't have a lot of time to prepare, so we quickly threw up some wooden barricades near the treeline. When we heard about the size of the force coming our way, and that those vicious Hessians were leading the way, well, I'll tell you that the mood was sumthin' a lot worse than tense. Our last order was that we had to hold the line here at all costs—and I believe they meant it. Not many of us thought we had much of a chance of stopping them here as they were said to be—as usual—better armed and trained, and greater in number. That "all costs" part of the order meant it was most likely the end fer the whole lot of us, and we all knew it. We all feared that we would soon be sleeping forever in the cold Connecticut earth. If any of us did manage to somehow survive their attack, we knew we'd most likely end up starving to death in a filthy prison ship in New York harbor.

Seb, who normally never talked to the officers, asked to speak to the colonel that day and that must be where they came up with their plan. I saw Seb and Thomas Giddings get in a supply wagon, and they rode off to Seb's house, which I heard was about six miles distant.

While some of us tried to sleep and others stood picket

duty, you could hear a large detachment of men digging up mounds of dirt and working hard around that big rock. At dawn, damned if there warn't a little earthen redoubt on and around that rock complete with a makeshift flagpole showing off our colours. The detail had strengthened it with some wood planks as time allowed, but it still warn't much to look at. There were also some shallow trenches dug right in front of it.

Sometime in the night while I was on picket duty, I saw Seb and Giddings come back with that wagon carrying a big wooden barrel of what turned out to be whale oil. I heard later that even though Seb's dad had died a couple years back, he had left Seb and the family a barrel of that valuable whale oil to use and sell as they saw fit.

We didn't have long to celebrate the founding of our new defiant redoubt. After a quick breakfast mess in the early morning, things turned serious.

The Redcoats were spotted on the opposite side of the field, led by their advancing units of Hessians. Their various units wheeled into formation like a finely tuned machine and stood there motionless like bright red and blue toy soldiers. We could hear some officers barking out orders, and then they started bombarding us with cannon fire. We knew they would start to advance en masse soon thereafter.

You could tell how ginned up they were about our colours flying proudly from our redoubt, as they concentrated most of their fire there. That bit of pique we caused sure saved a lot of us gathered at the treeline well behind the rock, I can tell ya.

I don't know how they survived, but our colours and the men in that outpost somehow made it through most of that barrage. Every once in a while when there was a brief lull, the few men in there would pull on the rope to make the colours flap more boldly, and you could hear them yelling taunts at the enemy. We all joined in with them yelling when we could, too. Boy, that made them Redcoats and Hessians madder than hornets and sure enough they committed the bulk of their advance force to march straight at that outpost.

The bombardment had slowed down as their men advanced, and now we waited fer our turn to give them a good volley. The colonel had ordered us to wait until they reached or got past the redoubt so we could really hit them hard. Hundreds of them advanced on us in tight formations, with a massed up bunch of them heading straight fer the outpost. The majority of the Redcoats and some Loyalists were back at the end of the field in reserve. When the advancing Hessians were about 100 yards out from the outpost, we noticed a few of our men's hands holding big jugs come over the outpost wall and start pouring some liquid into the trenches below. They managed to pour a lot of it quickly. Soon the smell of that whale oil was thick in our nostrils, as the wind blew it right into our faces. Horrible stuff that I'll never forget the smell of—made my eyes water sumthin' fierce.

The four men in the outpost, steady hands including Charlie Jerviss and Billy Moorehouse, suddenly stood up over their wall and fired a volley at the first group of Hessians, and then Billy and Charlie reached down to pick up two lighted torches. Wouldn't ya know it, but right at that moment the damned British artillery found the range and got a lucky barrage right on the men when they were most exposed. The balls hit in quick succession and after the smoke cleared, we saw in horror that the whole lot of them had been dispatched. The lighted torches still laid thar right next to their shredded bodies.

Afore anyone could utter a word or plan sumthin' else, I saw Seb get up from our treeline position and race toward the rock and outpost. I never saw anyone run that fast afore or since, and it's a good thing as the Hessians noticed him, too, and started fixing their fire on him. He made it somehow to the outpost just as the first dozen or so of them were climbing over the rock. Many others were following and walking through or around those trenches. The next thing you know came a torch spinning through the air that landed smack in the middle trench right below the rock ledge. That started off a massive reaction through all those trenches, and they caught fire quicker than lightnin.' You could hear them Hessians there start screaming and then the outpost isself erupted into a massive fireball of flames. There must have been plenty more jugs of that whale oil in there that Seb lit up.

That fireball was sumthin' you can only imagine when you think of the depths of hell isself, I'll tell ya. There was a massive loud whistling sound, and then a mess of big, flaming red waves of fire engulfed the area. I imagine it would be like if you got caught out in the middle of the ocean during a Nor'easter. I never seen its like again during the rest of the war nor since. The dozens of Hessians on or near the rock vanished into those waves. A good many of those Hessians in the trenches were burned up completely, while others were still alive fer a bit, but barely. Those survivors were the unlucky ones, lemme tell ya, because I heard them screamin.'

After we got over our initial shock at the firestorm, the

colonel ordered us up and we all discharged a lethal volley at the remnants of the advancing unit still standing upright. Then we set off full of energy after the retreating ones and their reserves behind them.

I remember coming across a couple of them wounded Hessians and they was mutterin' sumthin' I can still imitate despite it being in German. Someone told me later that it was probably *Flammen der Hölle*, which means *flames of hell*. They was all burned pretty badly, lying on the ground like babies and crying, and I actually felt sorry fer them fer a moment. Then I remembered how some of their kind would casually bayonet surrendering comrades of mine at earlier battles, including my friend Henry Allston, and I got over it and shortly put them out of their misery.

I should note here that in the years after the conflict, I did hear reliable stories that some of them Hessians stayed in the new country and made quite a favorable impression on their neighbors. It's likely true that a decent portion of them was good people just fighting on the wrong side. They sure were a tough fighting enemy, though. I can certainly tell ya that from experience.

As quickly as it began, the rout was compleat. The Redcoats and Loyalists in reserve had no stomach fer a fight after the massacre they witnessed. We gave 'em one more volley and continued our determined charge, and they retreated like scared rats. We collected more than our share of dazed prisoners and watched the rest of them scurry as quickly as they could back toward Danbury. It was as compleat a thrashing as I can recall ever experiencing during my time in service.

Right after our charge, someone found Seb's spectacles partially burned and twisted up in the grass in the cow pasture and handed them to me. They had been blown pretty far by that massive explosion. We never found a trace of Seb other than that.

When things had settled down a bit, the boys gave a great "Huzzah!" to the colonel and jeered the Hessian and Redcoat prisoners. However, when I held up Seb's mangled spectacles a hush quickly fell over our men. I remember saying sumthin' like "Seb's gone, but dammit he made the difference…" or some other feeble words that tried vainly to capture all that he meant fer us. Someone tried to start a cheer fer Seb, but we was all too depressed about losin' him to yell very loudly. I seen many hardened soldiers with tears streamin' down their cheeks lemme tell ya.

General Washington hisself—what an impressive figure he cut on that beautiful chestnut colored horse—came by a few days later and personally commended our unit. I really wish Seb had been around to see that powerful tribute because I know he really admired the general.

There were more battles to come, but that one really was a turning point fer us. After that battle, we really thought we could beat them Redcoats and Hessians and damned if we didn't do it in the end.

I think that's about all I can really say about that particular tale. Maybe some of the details ain't exactly right, but I explained them as best as I could more than fifty long years after it all happened. Believe me, especially you young bucks, at my age it's sometimes hard to remember what I ate fer breakfast.

I should also tell ya that Seb's mama went to her eternal reward maybe 20 years back, and she went ahead and bequeathed me his bag of treasured books and some other personal things. She also placed his crumpled spectacles in the bag right on top of the stack of books. She sent me those things because I was the poor basterd that volunteered to tell her the sad news about her heroic son and return his personal effects. I guess that's why she remembered my name and knew that I settled nearby.

I tell ya, when I saw Seb's books and personal things again after all the years gone by, I broke down and cried like a little baby. The whole damned war all came rushing back to me just like it were yesterday. The worst part of the matter was feeling that awful pain of losing Seb and some of the other boys all over again. But then I remembered the happiness Seb done brought me and the fellas, and the greater good he and them others were responsible fer, and it eventually soothed things somewhat in my soul.

I ended up giving all of it to a library company shortly thereafter. Not sure what them fine folks did with his personal things, but I take some comfort thinking that people are still reading some of his books to this here day. They most certainly contained a right lot of wisdom that would be useful fer folks. I should add that Seb was always quick to point to his bag of books and mention his pappy whenever any of us seemed too impressed with his clever words.

If you ever do go up to the rock, take a careful look and you can still see where that explosion took off pieces of it and some darker portions where the flames scorched it. That will bring the story even more to life fer ya.

I hope those of you who take the time to read this letter or the fella's newspaper story about Seb's Rock will pause fer a moment to think about what he and a lot of good boys and men like him sacrificed fer you and yours.

Maybe the next time you pass by a cow pasture or a field with an interesting looking ledge, knoll, or group of trees, especially in the parts of our great country where there have been conflicts, you'll stop to consider what might have happened there long afore you were on this here Earth. Some of them places have official memorials, but a lot don't. I know Seb, with all his attention to reading and larnin', will be happy wherever he is, knowin' he got you to thinking and wondering about the people, places, and events that helped shape your lives.

Humbly submitted,

Mr. Isaac C. Barton
Redding, Conn.

MY TWO CENTS

Mickey Zweifel grimaced as he looked down at the half-crumpled ATM slip in his rapidly moistening right hand. The numbers sneered up at him in slightly smudged print: *Current Balance $.02, Available Balance $.02.*

It was all just so unbelievable for Mickey. Fifteen years of backbreaking work and all he had to show for it were maxed out credit cards, overdue medical bills, and a whopping two cents in his checking account. The money he had borrowed from that world-class slimeball Rembourg had been a surprisingly short reprieve from the financial hell he was again living in. He buried his hands in his face because this was really the end. He didn't think about what this meant for him. As they had over these last tortuous years, his thoughts went immediately to his daughter Allie.

His little girl had been the one shining bright spot in what had been an uncommonly tough life. Mickey had grown up with a single mom in a working-class neighborhood in the Bronx. He was an only child who had received a lot of love from his mom—she worked herself to the bone for a house cleaning service trying to give them a better life. According to his mom, his father had been killed in a construction accident before he was born, but Mickey wasn't sure if that was all there was to the story. His mom did show him a few old pictures of the man she called Jimmy, but she would never get into the details of his death. The strange mixture of love and anger that came across her face as she looked at his photo suggested there likely was much more to the story. Mickey told himself he would look into what happened someday, but that day had never come.

His poor mom died shortly after his high school graduation—a victim of smoking two packs a day for thirty years. He would always remember how proud she was when she attended the graduation ceremony and stood next to him in his cap and gown. It was the healthiest and happiest he had ever seen her as she beamed with pride and affection. At least he had given her some joy and a reason to hope for his future.

A couple years after graduation he had married his high school sweetheart, Jackie, who was everything he could have wanted in a wife: loving, caring, supportive, and quite attractive. Things went well for them in the early years as Mickey found steady work as a heavy equipment operator doing construction jobs, and Jackie worked part-time as a sales clerk at a local jewelry store.

What Mickey didn't know was that Jackie was an alcoholic and had been since she had graduated from high school. She had told him that her dad had a drinking problem, and she had steadfastly shied away from drinking until near the end of their senior year. After that, Mickey only noticed that she sometimes drank one or two too many drinks on their infrequent nights dining out in the neighborhood. He figured she was just blowing off a little steam and shrugged it off. What he didn't know was that she did most of her drinking at home while he was at work. He probably would have been more suspicious if they had managed to spend more time together during the day, but that only really happened on Sundays.

When Jackie got pregnant, life seemed to be reaching new heights of happiness. Allie arrived after an uneventful pregnancy, and Mickey's heart overflowed with joy.

Things went along well until shortly after the end of Allie's first year. For some reason, Allie didn't seem to be crying or active enough and rarely made a sound. The doctors examined her and gave them the unfortunate diagnosis that Allie was suffering from some type of developmental disorder affecting her brain. The doctors offered different opinions about what the end result would be, but they all agreed that Allie would never develop normal mental capacity. She would need special care for the rest of her life.

One doctor spoke privately with Mickey and in hushed tones told him that he believed that Allie's condition was most likely caused by a combination of her mother's drinking and underlying genetic flaws. He had started to warn him about necessary changes if they were thinking about having more children, but Mickey had angrily interrupted him and defended his wife. He demanded an apology from the doctor, but the man only looked sadly away without responding. Mickey slammed the door on the way out of the doctor's office and loudly proclaimed to everyone in the waiting room that he would be switching his pediatrician that day.

When he talked later with Jackie about Allie's condition, he was stunned when she burst into tears and confessed that she had occasionally been drinking while pregnant. Mickey was furious at first, but after he witnessed the heavy sobbing wracking her body, he could only hug her and try to comfort her as best as possible. Her self-inflicted punishment and guilt were far worse than anything he could do to her.

"We'll take care of her, baby. Don't you ever worry about that," he told her with a firm, determined voice, but his whole body shivered as he thought about their scary and uncertain future.

After their new doctor recommended various drugs and special treatment centers for Allie, Mickey started working extra shifts to pay for their enormous cost. He even moonlighted on some nighttime projects where teams of similarly desperate workers would tear down condemned buildings. The salvage company gave them some basic protective equipment, but Mickey and the others still inhaled all kinds of ancient dirt and dust as they worked. He went home with his clothes reeking and covered in paint, dust, fibers, and whatever else was contained in the walls of condemned buildings.

At the same time, when he and Allie needed her the most, Jackie started to withdraw into a painful world of depression and alcohol abuse. She got fired from her jewelry shop job for showing up late too often and was even accused of embezzlement—although they never proved those allegations. Most days Jackie could be found on their increasingly ratty old sofa in front of the boxy television. She spent her time like a zombie, watching bad daytime programs and eating junk food. Mickey also knew that she often snuck in some daytime drinking, usually guzzling down cheap wine or beer. This happened while he was away struggling to keep them afloat. By the time he got home, she had normally fallen into their bed in an alcohol-induced stupor.

Mickey, who was as exhausted and old as a young man could feel, had tried to get Jackie to go to counseling and turn her life around. "Do it for Allie, if you won't do it for yourself or me," he pleaded. Her usual response was only to start sobbing and cry out, "Haven't I already suffered enough? Just give me a little more time to get over what I've done. I just need a little more time. Please …" Then she would throw herself onto the bed or the sofa and cry until her throat sounded hoarse. The sobbing only stopped when she mercifully passed out.

Mickey shifted his focus away from Jackie to taking care of and entertaining Allie. Even though she was mentally impaired, Mickey did see the light of life in Allie's eyes. Once in a while, if he was lucky, his constant wriggling of stuffed animals and toys and his funny voices would get her to smile and laugh just a little. Those moments were what he clung to during his constant backbreaking and soul-crushing times at work.

Less than a year later, Jackie was gone. Despite her protestations that she wanted to try to get herself better and be a real mother and wife, she simply ran out of time.

Mickey had gotten the awful call at one of his construction jobs. The normally mean and uncaring foreman had handed him the phone with some awkward compassion in his face and voice saying, "Uh, Zweifel, the cops are on the phone and wanted to talk with you. Something about your wife, they said."

The cops had requested he come down to the station, and Mickey knew that his world would never be the same.

They had found Jackie dead in an alleyway not far from their apartment. She was intoxicated and had frozen to death. The detective's theory was that Jackie had left their apartment to get some wine at the local convenience store. She had begun consuming it while taking a shortcut back home, slipped on some ice or something, and fell hard against the brick corner of an apartment building. She wasn't discovered until later in the evening when temperatures had dipped to near zero with the wind chill factor.

Mickey fought against the growing darkness as much as humanly possible. He moved them into an even cheaper apartment and found a reasonably priced caretaker, Maria, to look after Allie while he worked. Allie's condition had improved somewhat because of Maria's attention, along with Mickey's fawning over her in every free moment. He had also saved some money and gotten the best health and life insurance policies he could afford. He felt much better knowing Allie would be well taken care of if anything happened to him.

Allie had turned into a cute little girl with an ever-increasing amount of personality. She could now say a few phrases, such as "Love you, Daddy!" and "Daddy, play please!" With some extra determination, she could also say, "Hug now!" These phrases were always distorted in some fashion, but they sounded like divine music to Mickey's ears.

The doctors said that Mickey should start considering

sending Allie to a special school that could help her develop her full potential. They gave him some brochures to look at, but he could never get past the outrageous prices they all charged. He also still had to pay for all those expensive medicines and for Maria. He told himself with all the confidence that he could muster that he would think of something.

Mickey's world changed abruptly again when he was laid off at the construction site, and he quickly found out that nobody else in the area was hiring. He started to burn through their savings as he desperately looked for a new job. The only positive things about his new situation were that he could spend more time with Allie and save some money by cutting back on Maria's hours.

Things started looking up a bit more when a friend on his last worksite, Harry, texted him that there was a big apartment complex project starting up in 4-6 weeks, and he had the inside track to get on the crew. He promised he would get Mickey in as soon as it started. Mickey was relieved, but he now had to figure out how to bridge the gap until that job started. As it was, he was down to enough savings to cover their living expenses and Allie's medicine and therapy for only the next couple of weeks, if they really pinched pennies. He had to figure out something to cover them until that job started.

Mickey came up almost empty on borrowing from friends. Harry was the only one who lent him anything, and $100 wouldn't make any real difference.

He then decided to go somewhere where there was the possibility of making some real money: the nearby OTB location. He was no expert gambler, but he thought he knew enough about horse racing to at least make a little money. After being burned in his first few races and quickly losing $300, he was considering whether it was time to go for a long shot. That was when he bumped into Fred Rembourg.

Rembourg was just a little over average height, but his stocky build made him appear bigger and more menacing. It was hard to tell how old Rembourg was because he wore a fashionable striped hat that covered his balding head and any facial wrinkles were hidden by an immaculately trimmed salt and pepper beard. Despite the careful trimming, something about the beard still seemed wild and menacing to Mickey—maybe it was its thickness that looked like it could swallow you whole. Rembourg also had piercing blue eyes that would have made him almost handsome if his other features were equally as pleasant. However, he had a pug-like nose and thin lips that didn't match well with his oversized teeth. He carried himself gracefully and confidently in a suit that was well tailored but not too showy. He had quickly sized Mickey up as an amateur gambler who looked desperate and lost.

At first, Mickey thought Rembourg was just another degenerate gambler (albeit nicely dressed) with a typical unbeatable system, which would eventually work after decades of perfecting it.

"Hey there, Sport, if you want my two cents," Rembourg began innocently enough, "I would go with Dark Angel in the fourth race. I know his record doesn't look like much, but they've been getting some rain at Belmont and that horse is a real 'mudder.' " He smiled and gave Mickey an uncomfortably hard pat on the back, "Don't bet the farm, but I'd give it a shot. He's paying 6 to 1."

Something about the way the man looked at him made Mickey's skin crawl. "Uh, thanks for the expert advice, pal, but I'm going to head home before my luck gets any worse," Mickey answered.

Mickey became even more uneasy as he saw Rembourg's greasy smile disappear, and a goon the size of an NFL lineman stood up from a nearby chair and headed their way.

"Listen here, Sport," Rembourg said icily, "I might never have gotten good grades in school before I was kicked out, but one thing I could always do better than anyone was to read people. I'm especially good at telling when someone's on a losing streak. Call it 'loo-adar' for loser radar if you like," he said laughing at his own joke, "and I'm getting a major reading right here on top of your bony ass."

Mickey gasped for a second and looked around to see if he could somehow get away from these scary individuals. "Look, I—" he began but Rembourg grabbed him tightly by the arm and cut him off sharply saying, "No, you look, Sport. I'm not going to hurt you and neither is old Brucie here." Rembourg's greasy smile returned abruptly and the huge goon took a couple steps back and turned around to face the monitors above. "What I'm going to offer you is a way out of your current loserdom. Why don't you sit over here with us and listen to what I have to say." He straightened his tie and continued, "If you don't like my proposition, you'll be free to go on your way back to whatever hellish life you're living. Hey, if you don't feel like even hearing my reasonable offer, you can walk out that door right now. No skin off my beautiful nose. Don't worry. Nothing is going to happen to you in here with all the boys in blue hanging around." He motioned to a couple of bored cops standing near the betting windows. They were casually drinking coffee as they observed the gambling crowd. "Okay, Sport, what do you say?"

Mickey had listened to Rembourg and listened hard. His pathetic attempts at gambling had been futile. Mickey's assets were rapidly dropping, and his bills were mounting every day. Maybe this guy could help him stop the bleeding until he really turned things around in a couple of months.

At the end of what seemed a logical enough discussion, the men came to a handshake agreement on a $25K loan. Mickey figured that would be enough to pay off the upcoming round of medical bills and their expenses for at least the next 3-4 months. Yeah, he would have to pay Rembourg back $8K every month for the next five months starting the end of the next month, but that seemed fair enough. It wasn't a good loan term by any means, but no bank would be offering him a loan at any rate in the near future. Harry had guaranteed he could get him a high-paying job with overtime at the new construction site downtown next month, so he felt confident he could pay the loan back and turn things around. Rembourg was definitely scum, but Mickey didn't think anything would go wrong as long as he made his payments on time.

Mickey used some of the borrowed money the first month and kept things going reasonably well. The construction job had actually started early, and he was earning some desperately needed cash. He worked tons of overtime and the cash poured in.

At the end of the month, as instructed, he met Rembourg outside an Indian restaurant called Tail of the

Tiger in Hell's Kitchen and paid him back the first installment. Mickey was a little unnerved to see big Bruce there along with some other muscle sitting at a nearby table. The other men glared at him when he looked over. Bruce eyed the transaction with his customary blank face while Rembourg used the opportunity to praise and insult him at the same time.

"Hey, Sport! Nice to see you here on time and without a light envelope. Maybe my loo-adar is starting to malfunction a little as I get older, huh?" He laughed heartily, and some flecks of his dinner spat out and flew around their table. One particularly big chunk hit Mickey under his right eye. Mickey caught a whiff of some exotic spices as Rembourg continued talking, "Just think, only a few more to go, and we won't have to worry about charging new fees or extracting, I mean, collecting any penalties either." He laughed some more, and then his smile abruptly vanished. "Just make sure you're here next month and the ones after that, and it will never come to that."

Mickey nodded his head appropriately, and Rembourg quickly changed the subject, "Why don't you grab some *Murg Madras*? These guys make the best I've ever had. It's definitely some spicy chicken, but it melts in your mouth. You look pretty pale, and this stuff will give you some color real fast."

Mickey stuttered an answer, but Rembourg waved him off with a stony look saying, "You have a nice day, Sport." Mickey got out of there as fast as he could, almost tripping over one of the Indian servers.

On his next brief meeting with Rembourg, Mickey noticed some goons carrying a limp body out the back door to the alleyway. He purposely looked away to avoid seeing any disturbing details. Rembourg seemed happy Mickey had seen what was going on as he smiled and said, "Just keep them payments coming, and you'll never have to worry about unpleasant things like that, Sport."

About a week after his third restaurant meeting with Rembourg, Mickey noticed that he was growing weaker at work and had frequent shortness of breath. He soon found himself physically incapable of doing any more overtime work and took the corresponding hit on his finances. He fought through the weakness for another week willing himself to make every penny he could. When he finally dragged his beaten-down body to the doctor, he couldn't believe the diagnosis.

The doctor could barely look Mickey in the eye as he told him that he was suffering from aggressive malignant tumors in both lungs. If they had discovered them sooner, there would have been a small chance of treatment working, but now …

After Mickey got over his initial shock, he steadied himself and asked the doctor, "So how long do I have?"

The doctor sighed and looked down. "I think you might have six months, but the last few months are going to be very tough on you and your family. Take the time to get your affairs in order and prepare everyone as best you can." The doctor softly put his hand on Mickey's shoulder, but he didn't notice it as his eyes stared down at the shiny examining room floor.

Things took another turn for the worse when his buddy Harry told him the foreman wanted him gone the next day. "I tried my best, Mickey, but everyone's noticed that you aren't pulling your weight anymore. Lou told me you need to be gone today. He'll send your check to you. Is there anything I can do? What the hell's wrong with you anyway, man? You look terrible."

"Thanks for helping, Harry. You did what you could." Mickey tossed his protective helmet and goggles to Harry and struggled to make it home without passing out on the sidewalk.

A week later Mickey was back at the Indian restaurant, wiping his hands nervously on his jeans before walking through the door. He thought, *Why did time have to go so fast, especially when he had so little left?* He knew it wasn't going to be pleasant with Rembourg, but things went even worse than he had feared.

"Hey, Sport, on time again! Is that four in a row?" Rembourg put down his bottle of Kingfisher and motioned for him to come his way. "I'm really going to have to fix my loo-adar or stop drinking this Indian brew." He laughed loudly, and Mickey smelled the ginger on his breath.

"Uh, Mr. Rembourg," he coughed and then felt faint. "I've got most of it, but uh, some unexpected things happened, uh and…I was hoping maybe we can renegotiate some of the payment terms or—"

"Oh, Sport," Rembourg interrupted and his evil face was back. "I really didn't want my loo-adar to be working, but I guess in the end it really can't ever be fooled completely. It obviously needs some recalibrating 'cause I actually thought you would be okay for a little while longer. Let's see what you've brought me." Mickey handed over the crumpled envelope and watched in dull terror as Rembourg expertly thumbed through the wad of bills.

"Light a thousand, Brucie. I guess it's not the end of

the world, but it is still unacceptable. Now, what are we going to do about that?" He waved his hand and Bruce and two other men stood up and walked over to Mickey. "Let's talk about some new terms in my office, shall we?"

The meeting in the office near the kitchen probably only lasted a few minutes, but it seemed like hours to Mickey.

Rembourg snapped his fingers, and the two thugs quickly grabbed Mickey by his arms. They pushed him onto a wobbly chair in front of a beat-up table with graffiti and all kinds of scratches and dents on it. "Listen, Sport," Rembourg said with an emotionless voice, "Life can be tough sometimes, and everyone always has a really good excuse. Well, a good excuse and five bucks will get you a hazelnut latte at Starbucks." He smiled after he said his joke, but there was no joy in his face, and then his blue eyes became even more piercing. "Sport, if I renegotiated terms with you, I'd have to do it with everyone, and then the whole fragile thing would come a' crumbling, tumbling down. I'm sure you can understand my position."

Rembourg then turned to his men and said, "Brucie, he's only light a thousand, so let's just do two to remind him to do better for next time." As Rembourg finished talking, the two goons pushed down on Mickey and forced his left hand onto the table. Mickey was so weak that they didn't need to exert much force to hold him and his hand in place. Bruce then appeared next to them and pulled out something that looked like a steel meat tenderizer. Without changing the expression on his blank face, Bruce calmly lifted up the device and swung down hard twice on Mickey's pinky. The pain was blinding, and Mickey literally saw stars in front of his eyes. One of the goons had cupped his hand over Mickey's mouth, so his agonized scream came out as a muffled groan. Bruce then swung down hard twice on his ring finger. At that point, Mickey almost blacked out as the shooting pain blinded him. The men let him go, and he softly groaned as he picked up his throbbing hand.

He didn't want to look down, but something forced him to through his pain-wracked haze. Mickey didn't wear his wedding ring anymore, but he knew he would never again be putting any rings on those two fingers. Both fingers had already begun to balloon up from swelling, but they were so grotesquely misshapen and broken that they were blowing up at strange angles. They didn't look like they would ever come close to healing right. He feared they might as well have been amputated for all the good they would ever do him again.

"Hey there, Sport." Rembourg's cheery voice came muffled through the fog in Mickey's head. He felt like his ears were clogged with a bad head cold. "We took it easy on you this time because we want you to still be able to work and get us what you owe. Now get back out there, and see if you can prove my loo-adar wrong—at least for a little while longer. We'll be pulling for you." He motioned to Bruce and the goons to get rid of him but quickly added, "As a show of good faith, we'll expect an additional thousand along with the full amount in two weeks."

The next thing Mickey knew he was thrown into the alleyway on top of some garbage cans. He struggled mightily to get up and staggered home nursing his aching hand.

The next two weeks for Mickey were like living in a horrible nightmare. He had trouble distinguishing reality from his ever more frequent hallucinations and feverish dreams. In a recurring one, he found himself trying to walk in sand up to his neck while being pursued by a huge, evil black sandworm. When he looked back, he saw the thing coming ever closer with an evil smile that looked just like Rembourg's. He could never escape it no matter how hard he tried to run. It always ended the same way. He would hear Rembourg's evil laugh and would take one last terrified look behind him. At that moment, another head would pop out from the slimy body of the worm, and this one had Bruce's dead-eyed face along with massive fangs. Mickey would always try to scream in fear, but sand would start to pour into his mouth causing him to choke and cough violently. Finally, he would stare helplessly in horror as the slithering Bruce head would dive down into the sand next to him and start violently chomping on his hand.

Once he felt the fresh pain in his dream, he would awake to find himself back in reality with his hand feeling as if it was on fire. He would also be coughing so hard that it felt like his lungs were going to shoot out of his mouth. These spasms wouldn't end until some nasty phlegm balls covered with blood dribbled out of his mouth.

Mickey struggled to hide his increasing weakness from his illness, along with his new painful injury, from both Allie and Maria. He tried desperately to think through the dark clouds of misery to find some solution that could save him and his family.

He left Allie with Maria on one of her rare visits and went out to get some air to try to focus his brain. He didn't have the energy to go too far, but he pushed himself to reach his favorite park and bench under a massive oak tree. This serene tree had always calmed him during his stressful life. He enjoyed looking at the intricate patterns of its branches as well as observing the activities of the dozens of birds and squirrels that called it home. On his most recent visits, however, he found no solace nor could he concentrate long enough to make any kind of decisions.

When Mickey returned to the apartment, Maria greeted him in the entryway. She firmly touched his arm and said nervously, "Your uncle and his friend are here for a surprise visit." She tried to smile, but Mickey could see the fear and doubt in her mind as she waited for his reaction.

Mickey's face initially betrayed his shock as he looked past her to see Rembourg and Bruce making themselves at home in his living room. Rembourg wore his big greasy smile and was chatting with Allie like an old friend on their junky gray sofa. He even started petting her for a moment like a dog. Bruce sat comically in one of their small thrift store armchairs with his legs jammed up near his hunched over chest. As usual, he didn't say a word and had a blank look on his face. Allie just stared at the two men with a curious look on her face, not understanding who these two new visitors were.

Not wanting to alarm Maria or, more importantly, scare Allie, Mickey calmed his face as much as possible and said to Maria in a remarkably steady voice, "Oh, yeah. My Uncle Fred said he would be in town sometime this month and wanted to come by for a visit. I completely forgot to tell you about that. I really didn't think he would actually come by. He's been telling me the same story for years."

"Oh, I see, Mr. Zweifel," Maria replied seeming somewhat relieved, but still not completely convinced. "It's always nice to see family, isn't it? Should I make them some dinner or a snack? They didn't seem interested in any coffee."

"That's alright, Maria. I think he wanted to talk about some important family matters and isn't probably in the mood for much socializing. Why don't you take Allie down to the park for a bit while I catch up with him?"

Maria seemed relieved that there was a simple way out of the awkward and confusing situation. She smiled and started gathering their coats.

"Hey, there's my favorite nephew now!" Rembourg shouted across the living room as he caught Mickey's eye. "Come on in and say hello to your uncle and meet my good friend, Bruce. You've got quite a cute little girl here and so well-behaved." After he finished saying that, he patted Allie's head vigorously. This seemed to scare her a little as she backed away and then ran to give Mickey a big hug.

"Love you, daddy!" she exclaimed, although the phrase was unintelligible to anyone but Mickey. He hugged her firmly but tried not to let her sense his concern.

"Hey, baby girl! I'm so glad you got to entertain Uncle Fred and his friend. We're going to talk about some boring grown-up stuff for a while, so you and Maria get to go to the park for some bonus playtime!" Mickey said this with as much enthusiasm as he could muster. Allie seemed comforted by his attention and energy. She smiled broadly and ran to Maria who quickly put her coat and shoes on.

As they were getting ready, Mickey was forced to pretend he was happy to see his "Uncle Fred" with a quick handshake and clumsy half hug. He then turned to Bruce with a phony smile screwed on his face and extended his hand saying, "Nice to meet you, Bruce." As Bruce's huge hand swallowed his, Mickey noticed that Bruce's facial expression had actually changed. He was smirking ever so slightly. Thankfully, this awkward and painful performance didn't go on very long, as Maria quickly took Allie outside.

"Well, Sport," Rembourg began, "now I can see why you were so desperate for that money. She's a real doll." Then his expression changed, and he said bluntly, "Too bad she's got you for her old man." He then crudely added, "That spic maid or nurse is pretty well-built, too. Are you getting any extra services from her?" he asked with a laugh while Bruce smirked again slightly. Mickey thought that Bruce was really loosening up today.

"Why the hell did you have to come here, Rembourg?" Mickey asked with a surge of anger that hid his growing anxiety. "I don't want them to know how bad things are."

"Now listen good, Sport. You were supposed to be at the restaurant yesterday with your bonus payment, but you never showed up. We figured you might need a reminder of your growing debt to us, especially about your overdue payments. We also wanted to emphasize that we are well aware of where you live and know your family situation."

"I don't know what to say," Mickey stammered. "I'm doing what I can, but I'm going to need more time."

"Oh, Sport. That's precisely the answer that guys like me hate hearing," said Rembourg with his blue eyes growing brighter and more intense. "But, hey, I'm not a monster, right, Brucie? That cute little girl has bought you a little understanding and just a little more time for repayment."

"Thank you," Mickey grudgingly spit out. "I'll get you your money."

"Oh, I know you will in the end. We'll make sure of that. But let's see what we can do to take care of your bonus payment, etc., while we're here, ay Brucie."

As Bruce stood up, Mickey's legs began to tremble. He didn't think he could take any more pain without passing out or worse. "Mr. Rembourg, please, I don't—"

"Relax, Sport," Rembourg quickly interrupted. "Just show me where you keep your jewelry and any other valuables. And make it quick before your daughter and that hot maid get back."

Mickey was both relieved and heartbroken at the same time. The only jewelry he still had was the gold wedding band that Jackie had given him and the modest diamond engagement ring and gold wedding band that he had given her. The latter two rings were still in the plastic bag the morgue had sent to him containing her personal effects. He had never had the heart to take them out of the bag and look at them. He motioned to the bureau in his cramped bedroom, looked down at the floor and said, "Top drawer, there's my wedding ring and a plastic bag in there. That's all I have left."

Rembourg quickly picked up Mickey's wedding band and then looked in the plastic bag nodding his approval. He then stepped into the bathroom and opened the medicine cabinet. He cracked a smile as he took in all the prescription bottles. "I'll take a few of these, too, Sport." Mickey's spirit deflated even further as he noted how Rembourg skillfully selected only the most expensive prescriptions. "Relax, Sport, I'll leave some of them for you and the girl." He looked at his modest haul and then at Bruce and said, "It's a start, Brucie."

Mickey thought about pleading to Rembourg to leave more of the medicine, but he knew it would be futile. Thank God, Maria kept a lot of Allie's medicine in her own bag. He hoped it would be enough to keep Allie stable until he could figure a way out of this ever-worsening mess.

"Ok, Sport. This will cover you until your next appointment at the restaurant in two weeks. You're lucky you had something of value here and that I'm an old softy for cute little girls." He looked like he was going to tell another crude joke, but he stopped himself for some reason.

He and Bruce headed for the door, but Rembourg halted suddenly and looked Mickey right in the face as he said, "You look terrible, Sport. If you want my two cents, you might want to book an appointment with my Doc— he's the best and won't rip you off neither." He then continued with a smarmy grin, "You're no good to me if you can't work, Sport, so take care of yourself. I'll leave Doc's card here on the coffee table—call him today. No offense, but you look like you could use some astronaut vitamins, animal steroids, or some other special medicine, and my Doc's got whatever you need. Do what you need to for that sweet little girl of yours. Something to think about, okay, Sport." He patted Mickey with contempt as he and Bruce pushed past him and left.

#

Standing near the ATM, Mickey jerked back to the present from his long, painful recollection of the terrible things that had led him to this pitiful point. He crumpled up the pathetic bank slip and let it fall onto the dirty pavement. He then wept violently for about an hour in an alleyway near the bank. After he had finished pouring out his frustrations, he suddenly felt calm and focused. He had formulated a plan to settle things as best as possible. The funny thing was that Rembourg's snide remarks and suggestions had led him to a solution. *It was really the only choice left.*

Now Mickey was standing in front of the Tail of the Tiger and feeling strangely alive yet calm and focused. He felt at peace for the first time in years and actually had something approaching normal energy. Mickey didn't know if it was adrenaline or some other chemicals flooding through his body, but he savored the first feeling of normalcy in quite a long time. He closed his eyes and held his arms outstretched with his palms facing up to the sun. Mickey enjoyed the feeling for a couple more minutes, looking to people passing by like some exotic holy man in a Zen-like trance.

Mickey had asked Harry for one more big favor, and he had come through for him. As Mickey had instructed, Harry had called the restaurant and left the urgent message for Rembourg. Mickey now saw Rembourg, Bruce, and a new hired hand coming out of the restaurant at exactly the time indicated in the message. Rembourg had his usual contemptuous smile stretched across his face with his big, sharky teeth gleaming, and Bruce looked like Bruce always looked. The new guy was shorter than Bruce but almost as stocky. He even smiled a little as he looked at Mickey, but it wasn't a smile that gave you comfort.

"Hey there, Sport, we got your 'important' message," Rembourg said with his usual arrogance as he approached Mickey. "So you want to discuss some new terms, huh? I'm glad you were able to get some help from your friend there. Maybe we can get back on the right track again, ay Sport? Why don't you come inside, and we can talk about it over a Kingfisher."

Mickey looked calmly at Rembourg and replied, "No, Mr. Rembourg. I don't feel too comfortable in there anymore after what happened last time. I'd like to talk about things with you privately and out here in the fresh air if you wouldn't mind."

Rembourg was taken aback slightly by the steadiness of Mickey's voice and his new strange calmness. However, it wasn't enough to noticeably alarm him. He turned to Bruce and the new goon and laughed heartily, and then he said with mock seriousness, "Mr. Zweifel has some important terms to discuss with me. Okay, I'll meet up with you boys in a few. Have a cold one waiting." He waved his hand at them as if to say "no problem," rolled his eyes a bit in annoyance, and then turned back to Mickey. "OK, Mr. Big Shot, what do you have to say? I'll give you about three minutes of my valuable time out here since the weather is really nice."

Mickey waited until Bruce and the other thug had headed back into the restaurant and then waved Rembourg to come to him. "Let's go over to the alleyway there as I've got to show you some of my payment in private—too many people out here on the sidewalk."

Rembourg grinned greedily saying, "I hope your friend really set you up with some good stuff like he said, Sport. Now, that's a real pal. It's hard to find guys like that anymore. Believe me, in this business, I would know. I'm just glad I don't have to escalate this to the final phase—it's happened a few too many times lately, probably because of the recent economic downturn or something. Let's check out what new stuff you got for me and get this over with soon, okay, Sport?"

They turned into the nearby alleyway, and Rembourg started to crack another belittling joke. He momentarily lost his breath as he was now staring into a snub-nosed .38 revolver Mickey pointed inches from his face. He tried desperately to regain his composure saying, "Are you crazy, Mickey? My guys will be back here any second. Why don't—"

Mickey cut him off abruptly, "Then we'd better get this show started now, shouldn't we?" He pulled back the hammer on the revolver and took delight as he saw Rembourg's cocky face and swagger disappear. "Hey, Rembourg, did your loo-adar read this reaction from this loser? Well, I'm getting a major reading right here on your fat ass!"

"Listen, Mickey, I know we can work something out if we can talk this over," Rembourg said as he licked his lips in desperation and put his hands up meekly in front of him. His eyes were wide as he pleaded, "I know you're a reasonable guy, maybe w—"

Mickey cut him off quickly with one hand extended in the air saying, "I don't think so, you disgusting slimeball! I've just got one more question for you, mister moneybags genius. How does it feel? You like being helpless and desperate with some bastard owning you, huh? Just stand there and experience that wonderful feeling for a few more seconds, you worthless, soul-stealing snake."

Rembourg started to whimper something in reply, but Mickey ignored him and got down to business before the thugs returned. He pushed Rembourg back with all the strength he could muster and then shot him in the stomach. Rembourg screamed in pain and shock and grabbed at the wound as he fell onto some dirty newspapers. Blood poured onto the pavement soaking through the newspapers, and Rembourg stared up at him in horror. Mickey was surprised at how easy it had been to pull the trigger.

Speaking loudly so that he could be heard over Rembourg's desperate squealing, Mickey said, "Hey Rembourg, Old Sport, I've decided to give you *my two cents*. It's my entire life savings!" He took two pennies out of his pocket, bent down, and jammed them viciously into Rembourg's mouth, which again reeked of some exotic Indian spices. The spices were now mixed with the smell of gunpowder and copper and produced a bizarre aroma. The loan shark gasped and clutched at his throat.

Mickey was surprised at the pure joy it gave him to inflict pain and discomfort on this sorry excuse for a human being. He thought that it might have made up a little for all the misery this monster had caused and also prospered from during his scum-sucking life. "Sweet justice for you, you puke," he said out loud, although he didn't know if Rembourg was capable of understanding him anymore.

Rembourg choked a bit more on the pennies, his bright blue eyes bulging with fear and disbelief. He gagged a couple times more, his face turned purplish, and then his eyes became fixed. Mickey shot him two more times in the chest for good measure, and now the loan shark was still. Rembourg's body lay contorted on the filthy ground with his head leaning against a garbage can. His purple face stared upward with an expression of agony and surprise.

After a couple seconds, Mickey could hear some yelling coming from the restaurant, and he knew that Bruce and the new man were now running toward the alleyway.

"I'm sorry, Allie, honey," he said with a quiet gasp through his tears. "This was the only way it could work. The insurance money should be enough to take care of you in every way. God bless you and keep you, my darling baby girl."

Bruce ran into the alleyway first, waving his gun wildly around. In his frantic state, he didn't notice Mickey, who had just ducked behind one of the garbage cans. He stared in shock at the stunning image of Rembourg lying dead on the ground with his grotesquely purple face staring up in confusion and pain.

"Hey, Brucie!" Mickey yelled out from behind the garbage can. As Bruce turned toward him, Mickey shot him calmly in the chest with the last three shots from the gun Harry had provided. He was satisfied to see Bruce's usual blank expression turn to disbelief and horror as he dropped in a heap and the life quickly seeped out of him. The other man had started firing now, and Mickey made no effort to hide.

Suddenly there was blackness, and then slowly came light.

WATERSHIP RISING

Wayne and Katherine Patterson stopped on the highway because they urgently needed to get more fuel out of one of the gas cans packed in the trunk. Wayne put the hazards on and pulled over to the breakdown lane out of habit, even though he knew the chance of someone driving by was extremely remote.

The pair had been driving for a few days from California after exhausting the resources at their remote summer camp near Yosemite. They were now somewhere in the beautiful prairie lands of a Great Plains state—most likely Nebraska if the last road sign they paid attention to was accurate. Their goal was to reach any city that might have a research facility or safe zone still in operation. Up to this point, they hadn't seen anything too promising, and the radio just continued to play static.

The couple had been eating decently from their own supplies, but they had both developed slightly upset stomachs, which they knew wasn't a good sign. They vainly hoped that maybe it was just some indigestion from their most recent MREs.

Katherine had tried to stay positive as she thought about their situation. They had both always been self-described "high achievers" and were determined to be survivors—no matter what level of crap life threw at them.

Before things changed, they had been part of the young, cocky leadership team at an amazingly successful tech start-up in Silicon Valley, and they weren't going to go down without a fight. They had honeymooned in Bali for God's sake! Their plan had been to cash out their stock options by 40 and spend the rest of their lives traveling the world. Well, as her dad had once memorably remarked, "If you want to make God laugh, tell him your plans." Katherine didn't know if God or her dad were laughing or crying at this point—maybe a little of both.

The pair had always had ambitious goals and were driven to succeed at all costs—and what was more important than their own precious, meaningful lives? That's why they had been smart enough to bring plenty of provisions to their camp and wait it out until somebody figured out a way to stop or at least control this unholy virus. The couple had also not told any of their colleagues where they were going nor requested any official leaves of absence. They had gotten the hell out of Dodge while others wasted their time wringing their hands about what to do.

The determined pair had lasted more than 18 months on their own up at their isolated retreat and had somberly watched as the world fell apart on their HD satellite TV.

The virus had progressed rapidly and panic along with it. Someone had dubbed this seemingly unstoppable plague the "Worldkiller" or "WK" for short and the name stuck with the media. Everyone around the world was united in one common feeling: their hatred and fear of this invisible and unforgiving killer.

Their satellite TV transmissions slowly but surely faded away, and then the couple heard nothing for a good while.

Now they were prepared to drive all the way to the Centers for Disease Control, which they had learned was somewhere near Atlanta. *What else could they do at this point?* So far on their journey, they had only seen a few solo survivors in different places rooting through ransacked grocery stores. Those few scrawny individuals had been near the final stages of WK, complete with the nasty face boils, so the couple stayed well clear of them. In short, things out in the world were far worse than they had feared.

They had filled up as many gas containers as they could from their reservoir at the camp, and their sleek, fuel-efficient car had gotten them this far without a hitch. They knew that with the power out everywhere it would be difficult to find any accessible fuel pumps. They would definitely have to somehow scrounge some more fuel in the next couple of days because their gas containers would only last so long.

As Wayne bent over to fill up the tank, Katherine noticed how baggy his designer shirt and skinny jeans looked on him. They both had begun to lose weight, and it was becoming noticeable. That was another bad sign.

"Sure is beautiful out here," Katherine said softly to try to take her mind off things. "You know, I wish we had taken that train ride across the plains like we talked about a few years back." She slowly turned around in a circle and said, "I really love how huge the sky out here is—and I've never seen all these crazy combinations of different colors. It reminds me of th—"

"Yeah, it's really something special," Wayne interrupted in a mocking tone, "Makes me feel like singing "Home on the Range" or some other cowboy shit. Hey, you know what, Kath? Maybe we'll even get lucky and find a couple of survivors in the next few hundred miles, and then we can get a barbershop quartet going."

He stared at her with a look of anger and frustration saying loudly, "The only problem is that we ain't going to be seeing any 'deer or antelopes playing,' that's for sure." As he finished his rant, he angrily pointed to some animal skeletons on the side of the road that were probably either deer or antelopes or maybe both.

"Wayne, really?" Katherine said as her voice choked, "I was just trying to be a little positive. Why can't you at least try sometimes, too?"

Wayne looked down for a second, thought about being a wiseass again, then said contritely, "You're right, Kath. I've gotta do better. I'll work on it and—"

He stopped talking as they both heard a low rustling sound steadily growing louder. As they turned toward the strange sound, it seemed like the multi-colored grass across the prairie land was running at them in slow motion. Soon they could make out a tidal wave of small animals running rapidly toward them.

"Oh my God!" Katherine exclaimed. "It's really true! It's just like they said on the news!"

"Never seen anything like this," Wayne said in a hushed tone. "There must be thousands of 'em."

The huge swarm of rabbits was soon upon them. There was a dull roar of clicking and grunting, which slowly subsided as the rabbits began to graze. Then there was an irritating sound of soft nibbling all around them.

The herd was composed mainly of domesticated breeds that must have been pets or maybe even test subjects back before things went haywire. There were Angoras, Dutch, and some huge ones that Katherine recognized as Continentals, as well as dozens of other breeds that neither of them recognized. There were also some wild brown and gray rabbits as well as hares. In addition, there were some interesting hybrids created by all the interbreeding in the herd.

The huge, diverse group feasted contentedly on the long grasses and wildflowers growing near the highway. None of the rabbits paid any attention to the couple while they chomped away on this delicious bounty. There was no sense of agitation or jockeying for position, as there was plenty of food for all, stretched as far as the eye could see.

Wayne spotted one rabbit in a nearby group that looked exactly like the little black, floppy-eared pet his sister had when they were kids. The cute little bunny's ridiculous name quickly popped into his head: *Floppy Freddy*. He had never much cared for that annoying poop machine when he was a kid, and he couldn't stand the thought of him now.

"Can you fucking believe this shit?' Wayne said in an exasperated tone of disbelief and anger as he glared at the throng of contented rabbits.

"Well, the experts on the news said they were likely the only animals that weren't affected by WK, although none of them really knew what was going on in the oceans." Wayne didn't seem to be listening as he stared icily at the herd, but Katherine continued anyway, "Nobody was even sure if the insects were gonna make it. The plants all seemed to have done pretty well, though, at least from what we've seen."

"Great for them!" he replied sarcastically and angrily continued, "I still can't believe this garbage. Christ almighty! Fucking stupid rabbits! Bugs Bunny's wildest dreams realized. I guess they must have taken that 'left turn at Albuquerque!' " He laughed weirdly in a way Katherine had never heard before and continued, "I sure hope none of them have mutated into killer rabbits like in that Monty Python movie!"

Katherine desperately tried to steer the conversation back to science. She didn't want to hear that laugh again and really didn't like the way Wayne's face looked.

"Well, the experts figured that rabbits must have built up their immunities through so many generations of lab testing. There's some delicious irony, huh? Their descendants sure reaped the benefits from all those dark times. Kind of funny when you think about it!"

"Yeah, fucking hysterical. I just wish I had a big shotgun like Elmer Fudd so I could get us some fresh 'wabbit' meat." The strange laugh returned and Katherine cringed.

"You know, they also predicted that this herding behavior would increase as they multiplied without any predators left." Katherine looked over at Wayne, but he just continued to stare with eyes that didn't seem right.

Katherine was really getting worried about Wayne but continued, "I remember someone on the news bringing up how they had basically taken over Australia way back when even with predators around. But, I really don't think anyone could have predicted this." She paused a moment, but Wayne still didn't respond. "I actually thought they were supposed to live in dens or warrens or something like that, right?"

Wayne finally replied with an eerie calmness, "The whole world is their warren now." He paused for a few seconds then continued, "No need to hide underground anymore, my bunny buddies. Things have definitely come up all aces for you little bastards."

He looked vacantly at Katherine and at the rabbits again, and his lips quivered weirdly. "Why couldn't it have been dogs or cats, or even pandas? Nope—'silly rabbits.' "

Suddenly he yelled, "Unfuckingbelievable!"

Wayne then popped the trunk using the button in the glove compartment. He pushed the trunk up, jerked open a small backpack, and dumped its contents onto the hood of the car. Out came a jumbled mess of sunglasses, pens, keys, and other useless things along with some of his formerly precious possessions.

Within the spilled out contents, Katherine noticed his gleaming silver phone and a black monitoring device that he used to wear on his wrist. Wayne had used it religiously to track his carbs and chart his runs, bike rides, and different parts of his strict workout regimen. She also saw his clip-on music player and the wireless headphones he had always worn while running and biking before things changed. The devices had all been the latest models, complete with the obligatory bells and whistles to satisfy any high achiever. None of the gadgets had been used for quite some time. Wayne picked them up and whispered, "All fucking worthless junk!"

He then angrily and wildly tossed them at the small

group of rabbits closest to the car. The phone and monitoring device disintegrated as they hit the highway pavement, and the music player and headphones glanced off the rear leg of what looked like a Continental.

The small group of rabbits darted away for a moment, but they showed little concern. The Continental licked at his leg for a few seconds and then shook it out to make sure it still worked right. Soon the rabbits regrouped and were back grazing at the side of the road. They were oblivious to the fragments of the state of the art technology lying around them.

Wayne then fell to his knees and started pounding the soft ground next to the highway in a desperate, fitful rage. After a few minutes of useless exertion, he laid on the ground exhausted. He held his face in his hands and sobbed violently. Katherine could only make out some of his words, as they were quickly overtaken by more sobs. She did make out one part of his childlike whimpering when he said, "It's a nightmare. Just please make it stop. Please. Oh God, please."

Katherine left him like that for a few minutes as she hoped it would be a helpful and desperately needed catharsis. Then she knelt down and hugged him. He hugged back tightly, and she said tenderly, "It's gonna be alright, Wayne. You'll see. I just know we're going to find somebody to help us—even if we have to drive all the way to Atlanta. Hell, we'll commandeer a boat and sail to Europe if that's what it takes!"

Wayne looked up with puffy red eyes and a snotty nose. He smiled and said softly, "You're still the best, Kath." After a little bit, he seemed to recover or pretended to recover some semblance of normalcy and exclaimed,

"Goddamned right we're gonna make it!" He stood up and quickly brushed himself off while he scowled defiantly at the nearby rabbits.

They both got back in the car and waited a bit to calm down and focus. The couple had been active in meditation and yoga back home, but it was getting increasingly difficult to find their centers. After a few minutes, they both felt their focus was where it needed to be to start driving again. However, neither of them could help themselves, and they both looked over at the rabbits.

Most of the group had eaten their fill by now, and a decent amount of them were now laying on different parts of the highway sunning themselves.

As Wayne started the car up, some of the closest rabbits nonchalantly looked their way. Katherine noticed that the looks the rabbits gave them were not really arrogant or mocking in nature. It struck her that those looks were more like the looks people used to give squirrels or birds when they walked by them—not malicious, but merely a look that said you don't really matter. She felt that the rabbits must now sense innately that humans were irrelevant—almost ghostly afterthoughts. The new overlords really didn't need to pay them any attention of any kind. Not for much longer anyway.

"You ready, Kath?" Wayne asked with a forced smile that was more reassuring than his last few wild grins.

"Damned straight! We're fueled up and ready to go. We'll find someone or something soon!"

"Now that's my special girl talking," Wayne said with what appeared to be some genuine new hope. He pulled the car back onto the highway and headed east.

Katherine tried to hide the strain in her eyes as she smiled at him and gently rubbed her aching stomach. She tried to relax by looking out the window and enjoying the majestic landscape surrounding them. She also reminded herself to avoid staring at any of the massive herds that they would come across—no sense joining Wayne in meltdown land. Katherine knew that it was important to keep focused and stay positive if they were going to have any chance.

Look on the bright side, she said to herself. *It could have been the rats.*

REDUCED

The company's blocky blue letterhead reflected up from the letter in Jason Stentin's hand oblivious to the emotional pain he was experiencing. The cold text underneath began, *Dear Mr. Stentin, we regret to inform you that today will be your last day at Xannocom …*

The well-groomed, sensibly dressed, and ever positive HR Rep sat quietly next to Stentin's supervisor while the uncomfortable and unexpected conference proceeded. The HR Rep displayed her usual practiced reassuring smile, but it definitely seemed a bit more forced today. The supervisor sat uncomfortably as he tried his best not to look directly at his now-former colleague.

Stentin stared down at the letter again and tried to read it through eyes clouded with welling up tears of rage, anxiety, and sadness. His first thought was *how could this be happening to him?* Maybe some of the slackers in the office would be picked off by this latest round of "Reductions in Force" but not him. He had always worked hard and was friendly with the right people…

"Are you sure there hasn't been some kind of mistake?" Stentin asked loudly with a strange look of bewilderment that startled the HR Rep, who had been through quite a few of these meetings recently. "I mean … I've always gotten great job reviews, worked long hours on many projects, and been a real team player. Could they have somehow messed up the ID numbers for this? It just doesn't make sense … I've been here almost 15 years …"

The HR Rep answered softly but firmly in a well-worn diplomatic response, "Jason, this is not about the quality of your work performance. This difficult decision was made to respond to the many challenges presented by today's economy. Unfortunately, because of the current poor financial performance of the company in this new environment, we have been forced to let some talented people go in an effort to right the ship. The company has made the strategic decision to concentrate on other industry sectors that don't match some exemplary skill sets, including yours."

She smiled sympathetically and handed him a manila envelope from her desk. There were plenty more envelopes stacked in the bright-colored bin, silently waiting for their turn to rain misery down on their intended recipients. She continued in her schoolmarmish tone, "Jason, today will be your last day at Xannocom. In this transition envelope, we have provided the details on your generous severance package along with the login information for some helpful software tools to assist you in finding your next career opportunity." She finished with a phony smile, and the awkward meeting was over before Stentin had even adjusted to his new reality.

The next couple of hours passed quickly with awkward

goodbyes, tears and hugs, and the somber collection of his office belongings into a few cardboard boxes and company tote bags. Not knowing quite what to do at this early hour of the day, Stentin soon found himself at his favorite local bar.

He was stunned and still couldn't believe the company had really let him go. He had always done his job exceptionally well, but that clearly wasn't enough anymore. As he analyzed the situation, he realized that maybe he was being unfairly penalized for not being a pathetic suck-up to the leadership team nor a selfish, cutthroat dick. Those were usually the types of people that survived these things.

The emptiness he now felt was as exotic as it was overwhelming. His mind now began to reflect on things and assess them even faster than usual.

He sat quietly on the barstool and pondered it all. How could they feed him that corporate BS as they patted him on the shoulder and told him to get out of their pristine corporate office with its ugly leased furniture, unattractive modern art, and fake plants? They had transformed him and other loyal employees into mere figures on a balance sheet. He felt insulted, powerless, devalued, hurt, and embarrassed. He had been reduced to this pathetic state for what exactly?

As he drained a beer and ordered another, he thought about who was actually responsible for this latest economic downturn and its resulting mess. There were so many.

He and many others were paying the tab for incompetent government agencies that forced banks to grant home loans to people who could never afford them with the misguided goal of putting everyone into a house.

Tons of people were suffering because of greedy Wall Street firms and investment banks that came up with creative ways to profit from these new regulations despite the dangerous bubble it was creating. The well-being of many families, including his own, was now in jeopardy because of self-centered company executives who fought tooth and nail to preserve their exorbitant salaries. Those conniving rats always left with massive golden parachutes even when their companies performed badly. Politicians from both parties were at fault for accepting political contributions and sweetheart deals from interest groups of all shapes and sizes and not providing enough oversight into federal agencies or the financial sector. Their election season outrage now rang hollow, and their proposed solutions would probably only make things worse. The entire political system was fatally flawed in ways too numerous to count.

Lastly, he thought of the typical American consumer who constantly demanded real estate that escalated sharply in value and cheap consumer goods—no matter what that meant for US companies and workers. This unrelenting desire for the cheapest prices also had done quite a number on quaint main streets that tried to survive with only non-franchise stores. The average American also had to take some serious criticism for always expecting constant high returns in the stock market—no matter what type of behavior those results required or encouraged.

In short, there was a shitload of blame to go around for this ungodly mess.

He continued to reflect on different things as he considered what to do in his new life. It occurred to him that although most people tried to do the right thing, there was a small but substantial minority who would always try to bend or break the rules to selfishly help themselves. Because of these greedy and immoral people, everyone else had to suffer. When he thought about it all some more, a wave of gloomy sadness enveloped him. He left the bar quickly, fell into his car, and was reduced to tears.

The next evening at home, Stentin was trying to briefly escape his personal agony by watching *The Godfather* on one of his movie channel's "Movies You Need to See" nights. He could tell it was a great movie, but his mind kept drifting back to his miserable situation. The one thing that jolted him out of his stupor was when Don Corleone muttered his infamous remark about making someone a convincing, message-sending offer and then what that grisly offer was. He suddenly knew what he was going to do. Reduced to its core, it would be something dramatic and memorable.

Stentin decided to regain some control in his life. He wasn't going to let them all win without a fight. His mind worked frenetically as it came up with a defiant response. He would gain a measure of independence from Xannocom and all the corrupt corporations, banks, stockbrokers, and politicians that had devastated his life along with millions of others. He would deliver his own clear message that there is only so much that law-abiding, rules-following people will take.

Stentin successfully hid what had happened from his family, but he did seem more withdrawn than usual. He tried to continue his normal routine for the next week and act as if nothing was wrong. He worked hard to control the anger and sadness that was roiling him inside, but he had become something different and dangerous. He had trouble thinking about anything other than what his brain's accelerated functions focused on, even while he slept.

He used his former training and his severance package to coordinate and execute his plan. During some covert nightly visits, he checked and double-checked the schedules of all the nighttime security and cleaning personnel at Xannocom headquarters. He needed to be sure about that information and would confirm it again visually on the scheduled night. He noted that the cleaning people finished up by 9:30 and that there was only one night security man in the building after 10; he was normally in a car patrolling around the exterior of the compound between 10:30-10:45 and would not leave the building if anyone were still inside. Sometime during that time window, Stentin would commit his symbolic act of defiance.

On his carefully chosen night, Stentin used a good-sized dolly to quickly stack the large packages in front of the glass doors at Xannocom's headquarters. He placed them right near the ugly modern art fish statue and fountain. When he had finished arranging things correctly, he explored his feelings further.

Stentin remembered missing school events, his kids' birthday parties, and weekend trips with their friends and family. He had also often neglected his wife when he came home exhausted from a long day. It had all been because he was trying to impress the right people at the company with his hard work so that he could continue his steady climb up the corporate ladder. He had always had faith that his family would understand in the end. All of their sacrifices were supposed to be worth it once he got to where he needed to finally feel comfortable.

He also thought again of all the company projects he had managed and contributed to and the obscene amount of revenue he had helped Xannocom generate. "For what?" he asked himself again out loud and didn't even bother trying to come up with an answer.

At precisely 10:42 PM, two weeks after Stentin's last day at Xannocom, multiple explosive blasts went off at their corporate headquarters, and smoke and dust clogged the air. The ugly building groaned as its pillars crumbled and its roof and glass walls collapsed. As the debris fell, there was an awful screeching sound of concrete falling against glass and metal. It reminded Stentin of a lost soul wailing on its way into the netherworld. He found that he liked that sound and felt some closure and peace after it eventually stopped.

His mind, however, continued to reflect and calculate at an unusually fast pace, and he had no idea when that would start to slow down.

Now there were only the usual nighttime sounds of light suburban traffic and some noisy crickets. He even noted a few fireflies blinking their greenish love signals in the air in the nearby woods. "Life goes on, I guess," Stentin said softly and smiled wryly while he waited for the police to arrive.

In front of him was a beautiful sight: Xannocom's corporate headquarters had been reduced to rubble.

NIGHT CLOUDS

DRUMMOND'S BUNKER

Manzino moved Drummond's lumpy corpse into the far corner of the freezer after he couldn't take the smell anymore. He hated to do it because that's where all the meat and perishables were stored, but it was certainly the lesser of two evils.

He had hoped that the climate control system in the bunker had reduced the humidity enough to slow down the decaying process, but it hadn't really helped. Drummond had been dead for almost a week now and was really starting to get ripe. Bacteria always persevered that's for sure, and they had greedily started to feast. Manzino didn't know how many people were still left up above, but he was confident that all the invisible creatures up there would also be doing fine for the foreseeable future. They most certainly would have a lot of dead flesh to consume.

Manzino had never liked Drummond much back when he was alive either because the guy was just too weird and paranoid. He also didn't appear to bathe too often, which made close encounters under the summer sun even more

153

unpleasant. Both men were firearms enthusiasts, or what some people liked to call "gun nuts," but that's where the similarities ended. Manzino lived a fairly normal middle-class life in a single-family home in the suburbs, even though he had been divorced and living by himself for almost three years now. Drummond lived alone in a trailer on a run-down farm on the outskirts of the city. Nobody knew what he got up to out there on his own, but he constantly bragged about his arsenal of weapons to Manzino and a couple of the other regulars whenever he saw them at the gun range.

Nobody at the range liked Drummond, but Manzino had always been taught to be polite, so he usually ended up being the only sucker that would stick around and listen to his ramblings. Drummond just never let up about bizarre conspiracy theories that you couldn't even find in the darkest corners of the internet, and every week there was a new one. Manzino had to give him credit—his brain certainly worked well on whatever strange level it operated.

Drummond seemed also to have a soft spot for Manzino, probably because he had been a combat medic in Iraq and experienced some nasty stuff. Sometimes Drummond would try to get him to talk about his time over there, but Manzino almost always found a way to change the subject—usually just by asking him about his latest firearm purchase.

One time a couple years back when the light was fading, there was just the two of them still at the range. Drummond had finished spinning his latest conspiracy tale when he casually mentioned that he was glad he would be safe if anything really bad ever happened. He looked around to make sure nobody was within earshot, then proceeded to brag to Manzino about a tricked-out underground bunker he had built and prepared for the end times.

"I'll be alright down there for however long it takes for the crap overhead to clear up, that's for sure, Manzy," he said with a grin that was even weirder than usual. He had then proceeded to blast away with his automatic shotgun before Manzino could ask any questions. Drummond never brought the subject up again, and Manzino figured it might have all been bullshit.

When everything went to hell a few weeks back on an ordinary Saturday afternoon, Manzino had panicked like pretty much everyone else. Strange warning sirens started blaring, and then some vague, frightening message played on the emergency broadcast system on TV and online robotically saying:

Attention. This is a message from the Emergency Alert System. This is an emergency situation. If you are currently located in an urban area with more than 500,000 inhabitants, please calmly evacuate to the closest fallout shelter—most likely a school, city hall, or other public building. Please go immediately to the shelter without bringing anything but essential personal items for a brief stay. This is not a test.

The message then repeated on an endless loop.

Manzino's frantic calls to the police and 911 were met with busy signals, and that's when he found himself panicking like a child in a thunderstorm. He started rocking back and forth in his favorite easy chair hugging himself tightly. He had no idea what was happening, but he knew it was something big and bad. He wasted a minute or two flailing around like that, but finally, his

155

survival instinct and training kicked in: A calm inner voice asked, *Where are you going to go, and what are you bringing with you?* He knew any official shelters wouldn't be worth going to it whatever was happening was as awful as it sounded. To be safe, he knew that he needed to get deep underground and fast. Then two words echoed in his head giving him hope: *Drummond's Bunker.* He smiled for a second then quickly got to work.

Manzino reverted to his military mindset and demeanor as he prepared to EVAC. He filled up his duffel bag with various canned foods and bottled water, toiletries, and a few changes of clothes. He also threw in a case of his favorite craft beer, his Swiss army knife, and his Glock with as many magazines as he had lying around. He thought about going downstairs to get more weapons from his secure gun locker, but he quickly rejected the idea—it would take too much time, and Drummond already had plenty of firepower with him. His inner voice returned with more urgency saying, *Get to Drummond's, and get there fast!* He stepped it up, and within a few minutes he was driving in his pickup on his way to Drummond's lair.

Luckily, Drummond only lived about five miles away because panic had definitely set in throughout their fair city. Manzino witnessed a bunch of fender benders and even heard some shots being fired as he swerved in and out of the desperate motorists. He had no idea where they were going—probably just trying to get the hell out of the city on the main route—, which didn't look like it was going to happen anytime soon. He pulled onto a dirt road that led to the outskirts of the city and quickly reached the private road leading to Drummond's property.

Even though he had never been there, he knew that

Drummond had inherited his family's small farm, complete with a dilapidated farmhouse and a rotting red barn that hadn't been painted in decades. Manzino also knew that he stored his huge collection of weapons and tons of survival gear in that barn. Drummond lived in a beat-up old silver trailer on the property, but by his own account, he spent most of his time in the barn. Manzino figured Drummond's bunker would have to be right near the barn for easy access. Manzino knew the rough layout of the property because Drummond had spent countless hours telling him (and only him as far as he knew) about how he wanted to make it into a more secure home base.

When Manzino pulled up to the property, he immediately went to the barn. To the right of it, he noticed a decent-sized mound of dirt with a rusty metal hatch on top of it. He reasoned that the hatch had to be the entrance to the bunker. Manzino found a rock nearby, climbed up the mound of dirt, and started pounding on the hatch with the rock—he didn't know how much time he had left, but it was definitely getting uncomfortable. Finally, after what had seemed like a week, but was probably only about five minutes, a gray periscope rose up from the hatch. The long thin device, looking like something more at home on a U-boat, fixed itself on him at eye level. Manzino waved frantically at the periscope and yelled, "Hey, Drummond! It's me Manzino and only me out here! Please let me in, man! I don't want to die out here! Please open up! Hurry! You know you can trust me!"

The periscope rotated around trying to confirm what he had said, and then the hatch slowly opened up. Manzino collapsed to his knees for a moment in relief, and then he climbed down the ladder into the bunker.

In their new subterranean home, Drummond had started out being pretty good-natured—considering what was going on outside—and spent most of the first few days showing off his fancy set-up that would keep him safe from all enemies foreign and domestic.

Manzino was definitely impressed with Drummond's handiwork. The underground accommodations featured five distinct rooms: two bedrooms, a kitchen, a living room, and an extra-large supply room where the power generators, fuel tanks, freezer, huge water containers, and dry goods were located. The rooms were sparsely furnished with inexpensive or worn-out furniture including a comfortable white leather couch in the living room. The couch had some rips in it that Drummond or the previous owner had clumsily repaired with duct tape. There were precious few decorative touches anywhere as it practically screamed, *No girls allowed!*

There was also a small bathroom attached to the main bedroom. It was equipped with a porta potty type of chemical toilet and a shower nozzle over a sink. Drummond emphasized that water was their most precious resource, so a short military-type shower once a week was the only bathing allowed. He had also placed containers of handi-wipes and hand sanitizers everywhere that he insisted be used instead of water as much as possible.

Manzino had also noticed that there were a couple of dirty steel trashcans in the supply area filled almost to the rims with pre-1982 pennies. He also saw mounds of pennies in other metal lockboxes located in strange places around the bunker. Drummond explained that he had been storing this huge amount of old pennies for their high copper content. He had planned to make a fortune when the government discontinued the use of them. According to him, when pennies were no longer used as currency, people were going to be allowed to melt them down and sell the copper at a nice profit. Drummond had a sad face when he explained all of this to Manzino. He noted that his careful hoarding of pennies would have earned him a lot of money if things had gone differently.

Drummond also had a shortwave radio and internet connection in the bunker. The internet connection lasted for just a few hours after Manzino arrived, and most of the radio traffic disappeared within a couple of weeks. There were agonizingly few clues to what the hell had happened, as most of the Ham radio operators they were in contact with were only repeating rumors, which they had heard from someone else.

Supposedly, many of the large and medium-sized cities in the US and many other nations of the world had been wiped out, most likely by nuclear strikes or something even worse. Nobody really knew what had happened or even who the aggressor was. Drummond, of course, had his favorite conspiracy theories to fall back on, but neither of them would most likely ever learn the truth about what had occurred. The main question that concerned them was when they would be able to venture outside again. Drummond said he was going to be making some tests of the air soon to try to determine when it might be safe to leave their underground fortress.

At first, Drummond had seemed to really enjoy Manzino's company and was happy to cook them good meals and watch episodes of *The Tonight Show with Johnny Carson* on DVD. This classic TV talk show appeared to be the only form of video entertainment he liked. To show his appreciation for Drummond's hospitality, Manzino always made a point to listen attentively to Drummond's commentary on everything from what had happened outside to his favorite guests appearing on the show.

Drummond was also a crossword puzzle fanatic and had stacks of magazines everywhere that contained old puzzles from the most famous newspapers and other sources. Manzino tried his best when Drummond asked for help on the puzzles, but it just wasn't his forte.

Manzino remained grateful just to be alive and apparently safe down in Drummond's underground sanctuary, although sometimes his imagination would rev up at night. He occasionally had horrible dreams that someone was bulldozing tons of dirt over the bunker and then paving a layer of concrete on top of them. When he woke up, he was always gasping for air. He was definitely getting a little stir crazy, but he did his best not to show it to Drummond.

Manzino also noticed that Drummond was getting a little moodier with him as the days passed by. He had, however, gotten a few nice days of "good mood" Drummond when he had helped him solve a crossword clue that had been vexing him. The clue asked simply, *One of Iraq's 19 governorates*, and Drummond had already written in the first two of its seven letters: Ka. His face absolutely lit up when Manzino quickly told him the answer of "Karbala." He smiled, gave him a pat on the shoulder, and exclaimed, "Great to have you here, Manzy!"

One night after dinner, Drummond had even boasted that they could last in the bunker for 8 to 10 years depending on how carefully they rationed their food and water.

Everything had been going along as well as could be expected when Drummond suddenly accused Manzino of stealing food. Things had gotten exponentially worse after that.

The exchange had been awkward and terrifying that night in the kitchen. Manzino had just taken a grape juice box out of the refrigerator for some late night refreshment. When he turned around to sit down, he found Drummond standing uncomfortably close to him.

"Enjoy stuffing your face last night, Manzy?" Drummond began out of nowhere with a weird, angry look as he angrily slammed a tin cup down on the counter.

"Ah … no more than usual, Norm, I'm not sure what you mean—"

"Don't you understand, you fool," Drummond cut him off sharply with his face bright red and the main vein in his forehead throbbing, "I've carefully rationed out all the meals in this facility so that I and any other occupants can achieve the highest duration of survival. You can't just have a midnight snack whenever you feel like it, understand? We have to maintain discipline at all times, or this whole effort is for naught. Do you get me?"

"Really, Norm, I didn't—"

Drummond waved his hand and cut him off saying, "Just promise me, my friend, that nothing like this will ever happen again, and we'll drop it, okay?" Drummond then brandished his favorite .38 revolver as he looked at Manzino with frightening intensity.

"Of course, Norm," Manzino choked out as some sweat beaded up and slowly dripped off his chin onto one of the crossword puzzle magazines lying half-opened on the kitchen counter. "I know I'm a guest here, and I very much appreciate and respect the rules of the house. No problem here at all."

"Great to hear that, Manzy. Outstanding!" Drummond replied. Then his intensity overdrive gear slipped back into normal and he smiled saying, "You know, buddy, I really want to find that episode where Robin Williams makes his first guest appearance. Pure comedy gold!" He slapped him on the shoulders and started looking through his stack of DVDs in the living room. He ignored Manzino and muttered to himself as he slowly examined a few promising-looking candidates.

Another weird moment occurred when Manzino had just finished relieving himself in the porta potty. He was surprised to see Drummond waiting for him on the cot as he came out of the toilet.

"Manzy, I heard you using a little water in there," Drummond said calmly with a stern look on his face.

"Norm—you scared me," Manzino said with a hopeful laugh. "Were you actually listening to me on the toilet?

"If you mean monitoring the water consumption level in this facility, then yes," Drummond replied without changing his expression. "I take water waste very seriously."

"Listen, I don't mean to be graphic, but things were a little nasty, and I needed a quick squirt of water to, uh …"

"That's what the handi-wipes and hand sanitizers are for, my friend. As you know, I've made sure we're well stocked with those." Drummond gave him one more stern look, patted him hard on the shoulder and said, "Just make sure you always remember that."

"You got it, Norm. Consider it a lesson learned in

bowel movement protocol," Manzino replied making an A-Okay sign with his right hand. He then flashed a phony smile to try to lighten the tension.

"Your turn to make dinner, and don't use any eggs tonight," Drummond responded flatly, and then he abruptly left the room.

The next few days had gone relatively routine, but Manzino had been shaken up enough by these strange encounters to start sleeping with his Glock hidden under his mattress.

Just when Manzino thought Drummond's recent bouts of weirdness had been a temporary fluke, and he started to feel a bit more normal, he had found something that made his skin crawl.

While Drummond was sleeping one night, Manzino had been scanning through a stack of the old crossword puzzle magazines in the living room. He had been hoping to find one that might be a little easier to handle. Hidden deep down in a pile, he had come across a promising one called *Crossword Crazy: Fun Puzzles for All Ages and Abilities!* When he pulled it out of the stack, a small green-covered notebook had fallen out of it onto the floor. On the cover was the word *NOTES* written in Drummond's crisp block lettering with a black Sharpie.

Manzino made sure that he could still hear Drummond's loud snoring while he peered inside the well-worn notebook. The first few pages listed some of the latest conspiracy theories Drummond had been spouting along with some recipes featuring canned pinto beans and freeze-dried food. Nothing seemed all that interesting until he reached the middle pages. In block letters there stood the official sounding heading *ALLOCATION OF*

RESOURCES with a couple strong underlines. After a few lines noting various amounts of supplies, there was suddenly an eerie entry: *COST BENEFIT OF M?*

The content below was short and to the point. *M offers the valuable skill of combat medicine and is tolerable as a companion. Solitary life, it must be remembered, can be trying at times for even the most well-prepared warriors.*

The next entries went on to talk about how to keep the porta potty working without clogging, and how to best monitor mold levels in a humid underground bunker. Manzino was about to put the notebook back where he found it when he noticed a folded up yellow sticky note on the last page.

The writing had shifted to blue ink and all caps and said, *FINAL ANALYSIS: M'S POSITIVES NOT WORTH RISK TO ALLOCATED RESOURCES. SUFFICIENT ENTERTAINMENT ON OWN. PRESERVATION OF RESOURCES FOR LONGER STAY IS TOP PRIORITY. TERMINATE M WITH EXTREME PREJUDICE WHEN OPPORTUNITY ARISES. EXECUTE PAINLESSLY IF POSSIBLE, BUT ACHIEVE OBJECTIVE AT ALL COSTS!*

Manzino felt faint as he slumped down on the couch, and it all hit home. Bottom line: he knew Drummond was borderline crazy but also efficient. If he planned something and wrote it down, it was going to happen.

Manzino knew he had to act fast to protect himself, so he immediately headed into his bedroom. As he dragged his hand under the mattress, he was shocked to feel only the coldness of the cot's metal springs. His heart raced and cheeks flushed when he realized with horror that Drummond had confiscated his weapon.

His brain whirred as he started thinking about other possible weapons. He knew that Drummond's arsenal was stored in a big locker in his bedroom under lock and key.

Get a knife from the kitchen! his faithful voice recommended to him, and he immediately acted upon this good advice. He scrambled into the kitchen and took the biggest steak knife he could find from the silverware drawer.

Manzino then started to formulate a plan to kill Drummond while he was still sleeping. He was just heading back across the living room when he was startled by a calm, condescending voice saying, "Manzy, was that really the best idea you could come up with? A man with all of your military experience."

Drummond was sitting on the leather couch holding his trusty .38 as he spoke with Manzino. Instead of the intense glare that Manzino expected, Drummond had a half smile on his face and actually looked healthy and in good spirits. "Why, I would have thought you'd have just smothered me with a pillow as I slept and been done with it. Relatively quick and painless and not nearly as much of a mess—at least that's what I've read in some of my literature."

"Norm, ah, I was just getting something to protect myself so we could talk this out. You took my gun for Christ's sake. What was I—"

"Manzy, I knew it would just be a matter of time before your ingratitude would take hold."

Drummond stopped smiling for a few seconds while he paused to think and then continued, "I had to fight against my usual good judgement telling me to get rid of you a while back because I did appreciate your company." He seemed genuinely sad for a few seconds while both men were quiet.

Manzino then piped up saying, "There's got to be a way we can resolve this, Norm. We might actually be the last two people left in the whole fucking world—right here in your bunker! Think about that! Do you really want to do this? I swear to you on a stack of bibles that I didn't do anything wrong."

While he pleaded for his life, Manzino's brain had switched into combat mode. The adrenaline was really kicking in now, and he knew what he would do. He wasn't going to let this psycho bastard slaughter him like a lamb without at least trying to fight back.

Drummond's grin returned as he responded, "Manzy, your concerns have all been noted and considered, but I've reached my final decision for the good of this facility." His eyes lit up as he continued, "You know, I'm actually kinda excited to finally bust my cherry like I've been itching to do for years. I'm sure you can relate to that with what you went through in Iraq. I promise it's all for the greater good and will be over quickly. I'm a damned good shot as—"

While Drummond blabbered on, he had slowly stood up from the couch. His gun had gotten a little heavy in his hand, and he had let it fall gently down to his side. Manzino took this opportunity to kick the beat-up coffee table in front of the couch right into Drummond's shins. As Drummond screamed in shock and pain, Manzino dove to the floor and crawled like a madman around the couch to try to get behind him to use the knife. Drummond raised the gun and fired once, but as he moved forward, his right foot slipped on the slick cover of one of the crossword magazines lying on the floor. His foot flew up comically, and he fell down hard on his back.

"You little sunuvabitch!" he screamed out while lying in pain. "You're making this hard—man, is it going to cost you!" He then sprayed a few shots wildly in the general direction of where he thought Manzino was.

Manzino wasn't listening in those few seconds while he calculated his next move. He knew there was no way he could stand up over the couch and use the knife without getting plugged. Then he noticed one of the heavy metal lockboxes loaded full of pennies sitting on the shelf right over him and slightly behind the couch. He turned over on his back and kicked the bottom of the shelf as hard as he could. The lockbox, which must have weighed at least 50 pounds, tumbled down right on Drummond just as he was beginning to get up. Manzino heard a strange popping sound and a loud gasp from Drummond and then nothing. After a few seconds of silence, he felt he had to risk doing something. He jumped over the couch with his knife poised to strike, fully expecting bullets to rip into him.

Manzino landed on his feet right next to Drummond, who wasn't moving. The lockbox was tilted over and wobbled halfway on Drummond's face. He still clenched the gun in his hand, but he wasn't going to be busting any cherries anytime soon. His nose and whole face had been dented in by the weight of the lockbox, and blood was gurgling out of his mouth. Pennies were scattered all around Drummond's head and body, some now covered with blood. With one close look at that smashed-in face and his experience as a combat medic, Manzino knew that Drummond was no longer a threat.

After a few more seconds of observation, he kicked the gun out of Drummond's hand and plunged the steak knife deep into his chest. He wanted to make certain it was over.

Manzino then went into the kitchen and took one of the cheap paper tablecloths, still stained from that morning's instant oatmeal breakfast, and covered up Drummond's disfigured face. "By the way, I hate the nickname 'Manzy,' you crazy fuck," he said and kicked the body hard about ten times just for the hell of it. He immediately felt much better.

Drummond had certainly been right about one thing: it would have been much better if it hadn't been so messy. He still managed to clean things up in the living room almost as good as new with plenty of bleach and elbow grease. He tried not to think about how Drummond had planned to take care of him when the time came.

After Manzino had given up on avoiding the storage of Drummond's corpse in the freezer, his mind tried to formulate when he would feel safe enough to open up the bunker hatch and toss him out. He now had plenty of time to decide on when to take that action, even though he was still disgusted by the image of Drummond's body lying near the frozen slabs of beef in the freezer.

After storing the body and decompressing for a while, Manzino started to turn his attention to some of *The Tonight Show's* best moments, since that was pretty much all he had for entertainment. He eventually also discovered one DVD featuring some classic Dean Martin celebrity roasts and began enjoying the hijinks on it. Manzino found that it was like opening a hilarious time capsule. He thought the old time comedians were a laugh riot, and he got a kick out of how everyone smoked like chimneys and got drunk during the festivities.

When Manzino wasn't watching the DVDs, he spent a

good amount of time trying to complete crossword puzzles. His puzzle-solving method was to fill in the difficult clues first using the answer key and then try to get the easy and moderately difficult ones without help. He had noticed that he was starting to enjoy it more, and if he didn't like the particular crossword puzzle, he had thousands more to choose from stacked throughout the bunker. He almost had the answer to the latest clue that was driving him nuts. The clue was *Up to the job*, and the answer was seven letters starting with Ca and ending with an E. There was no internet to look stuff up, so he was glad all the magazines had the answers in the back! He was definitely improving, and he had plenty of time to refine his skills.

Another pastime he had taken up was stacking columns of pennies into high towers and creating building-like formations. He also sometimes softly tossed pennies at thick spider webs to see if any would get caught.

Tonight Manzino was focused on watching *The Tonight Show*, which he increasingly appreciated. He found that fact amusing because he had never been a late night television fan, and Carson had been popular before his time. Johnny's announcer and sidekick, Ed McMahon, was also starting to grow on him. He also liked the sketches by the Mighty Carson Art Players and enjoyed Johnny's banter with Doc Severinsen and the house band. Then there was the thrill of seeing some familiar actors and comedians when they were just starting out. Watching actors like Tom Hanks and Meryl Streep as up and coming new talents was really a kick, and he enjoyed Jerry Seinfeld's first stand-up routines. The legendary insult comic Don Rickles in his prime was always a real treat, and he popped up in many episodes.

"Yes, sir!" Ed McMahon said authoritatively in his deep voice beloved by millions back in the day.

Manzino suddenly found himself a little sad that Carson's Carnac the Magnificent character, a fortune-telling mystic with a ridiculously oversized red turban, was reaching the end of his latest skit. Ed had signaled this as usual by saying emphatically that he held the last envelope of the routine in his hands, and the studio audience cheered in jest as they always did. Johnny obliged them with a particularly funny comeback, and the audience roared with delight.

Luckily, Manzino knew there would be many more episodes to follow. If he ever grew tired of his underground life, he also knew that his trusty Glock was lying comfortably in the top drawer of a kitchen cabinet.

"No problem. Just need to relax a little and take things as they come," Manzino said out loud with a smile. That night the ragged old white leather couch felt particularly comfortable as he stretched out his legs. He didn't even notice the duct tape anymore. All in all, Drummond's bunker was really starting to grow on him.

"Thanks, Norm," Manzino said, "You built one hell of a cozy home down here ... you crazy bastard." He raised one of his last craft brew bottles in salute to his benevolent provider and drained it with pleasure.

Just then, he heard Ed's hearty belly laugh in faithful response to one of Johnny's witty quips. It echoed perfectly down the bunker's concrete corridors with all its steel doors and compartments. Ed's warm laugh made him feel, for a moment anyway, as if he wasn't alone.

PICK SIX

Lenny checked under the couch cushions one more time to see if he could scrounge up enough change for a midday snack. His stomach was growling, and sweat had started beading up on his forehead as he lifted up the cushions and moved his couch around to explore every nook and cranny. As he shook the beat-up couch with more intensity, he finally heard the lovely jingling sound of loose change hitting the floor. He quickly looked down to search for his reward.

Tangled amid cat hair, paper napkins, crumpled receipts, gum, dust bunnies, and other unidentified food or dirt particles he found the grand total of 87 cents. *Not bad!* He thought with satisfaction. Combined with the $2.42 in his pocket, he calculated that he could get a couple of hot dogs or some other microwavable treat at his favorite convenience store. He casually brushed the motley mixture of refuse from the couch off his sweaty arms and headed out the door.

As Lenny walked outside, he noticed that the headache

that had bothered him for the last few days had receded to a dull, manageable pain.

He had been the victim of a drive-by attack one night last week when he was walking home. Some scary guys he had never seen before had jumped out of a car and started beating the shit out of him. Fortunately for Lenny, they had just started the beat down with their fists and didn't get around to using their heavy work boots to stomp on him. Within the first minute of the beating, Lenny had taken a punch square on the chin and fallen down hard, hitting the back of his head on the curb.

As he lay there in a daze, he heard the thugs talking while they searched through his wallet. They were at first annoyed that he only had a few bucks, and they were even more frustrated when they discovered, via his driver's license, that they had been pounding on the wrong guy. However, the men didn't offer Lenny any apology for this violent case of mistaken identity. They quickly sped away, leaving him lying sprawled halfway in the street.

After the attack, Lenny was taken to the nearest emergency room. The medical staff there patched him up, did some head x-rays and other tests, and pronounced him fit to leave the next day. His doctor gave him some extra-strength aspirin and told him to come back if he had any nausea or if his headache got worse. Lenny felt fortunate that he had survived his ordeal and gotten some good medical care even without any insurance. Aside from his diminishing headache, all there was to remind him of the vicious attack was a big bump on the back of his head and some scrapes on his hands and arms.

With a slight spring in his step, Lenny made the short walk around the corner to Pop's Market. Alonzo "Pop"

Martin and his son Walt gave him a nod as he entered, but they made no attempt to make him feel especially welcome. Lenny was a frequent customer, but he had never spent much money in Pop's, and there was nothing to indicate that this would be changing anytime soon. They also didn't like Lenny's overall appearance—unshaven, unkempt hair, and grungy clothes that he rarely changed. He also didn't bathe regularly, which you quickly noticed when he got within a certain distance. Pop wanted to attract wealthier customers from the up-and-coming neighborhood nearby. Having Lenny and others like him frequenting the place didn't help that cause.

"Hey, Pop!" Lenny said warmly, oblivious to their cool treatment of him. "Any new specials today? I'm really craving something tasty."

"Nah, just the usual good stuff," Pop replied without looking up from reading his magazine on the counter. Then he couldn't resist and said, "You splurging today, Lenny? Skies the limit, right?"

"I'm a rich man today, Pop!" Lenny said with his winning grin. "I don't have a lot of money, but I'm rich in friends and experiences, my man." Pop and Walt continued to ignore him until Lenny got down to business asking, "Hey, you still have the two dogs for two dollars special?"

"Take your pick, Lenny," Pop replied pointing to the relatively fresh hot dogs rotating in the reheating area of the food display. "Any two you want and all the condiments you want to go with 'em."

Lenny smiled and reached for some ketchup and relish packets—he loved that sweet mixture on his dogs. As he strained to get a few extra packets of each (maybe to snack on later), he noticed a fresh stack of lottery tickets on the nearby counter behind the protective glass. The tickets were rainbow-colored with *Vegas Slotmasters* written in bold letters on the front along with *Match three in a row for $100!!!* in big gold letters. Directly underneath this were three small scratch-off spaces. In smaller red letters on the bottom, it said *Only 50 cents to get in on the action!*

Lenny had never even thought about lottery tickets in the past, but for some reason, his eyes lingered on this set of tickets. "Is this a new game?" he asked Pop.

"Yeah, we just got 'em in today. They send us new games every now and again to test the market. I played a couple and didn't win anything. The price is definitely right though." Pop glanced over at Lenny and was surprised to see his normally cheerful, goofy grin replaced by a face at rapt attention. "Lenny, you okay, son?" Pop asked with a bit of concern.

Lenny was preoccupied with looking down at the tickets. He was stunned to discover that he could actually sense that one in the first stacked group of about 50 was a winner. He didn't know how to explain it, but the second ticket in the first stack had a glowing, blue aura around it, while the others had flat, gray auras. Pop's loud question quickly brought him out of his trance.

"Sure, Pop," he said softly as he tried to compose himself. "Just, ah, daydreaming of winning some big money, hahaha," he finished with an awkward, stuttering laugh and a smile that Pop didn't share with him. "Say, Pop, I'm feeling pretty lucky today. I think I've got enough scratch for the dogs and two big winners today. Give me two from that first little stack on the right."

Lenny piled up his meager stash of crumpled bills and

linty change on the counter in front of Pop. With a slight grimace of disgust, Pop rung up the purchase and pushed back some of the linty coins. "Good luck, Lenny. Hope you win big so you can spend more money in my fine establishment."

Lenny eagerly wolfed down one of the dogs smothered in ketchup and relish. As he wiped some stray ketchup and crumbs from his mouth, he mumbled, "I'll save this one for later," and wrapped up the other hot dog in a napkin. "Might as well give these babies a try right now." He purposely rubbed the boxes on the losing one first and acted a bit deflated when they came up empty. "Oh well, still got one more chance. Mama always said, 'ya gotta keep trying or you just be dying' or something like that." He rubbed the boxes slowly and deliberately and acted excited as the first two matched. "I think that's at least a free game, right. C'mon, just one more! YESSSSS!!!! 100 bucks!"

He grinned and handed over the winning and losing tickets to Pop, who stared at him a bit longer than usual. Pop was stunned when he looked down and confirmed that it really was a winning ticket. He quickly composed himself and offered his muted congratulations. "I'll be damned! Well, Lenny, it looks like you live under a lucky star after all. You want your payout now, son, so you can buy some more tickets?"

Walt piped up with a little more friendliness, "Keep riding that hot streak, Lenny. Congrats, Mr. Vegas!"

Lenny gave them both a broad smile and then said loudly but politely, "I'll take the money right now, Pop. I can use it to buy a few groceries here."

"Sounds good to me, Lenny," Pop replied as he slowly

counted out Lenny's money. "Just remember where you need to come to get your next tickets. Make sure to spread the word about how lucky this place is. Maybe you should move up to the big leagues with *Pick 4* and *Pick 6*, Mr. Big Shot. You could win some serious money then and make us all rich!"

Lenny happily took the money and proceeded to buy about $30 worth of much needed groceries as well as some of his favorite beer, which he could rarely afford. He had a big smile on his face as he left Pop's Market, but he noticed that his headache had now become somewhat painful again. He kept smiling, but he rubbed his head and walked faster to get home and take some of his aspirin.

Lenny sat in his apartment and happily looked at the money piled in front of him on his decrepit coffee table. He had cooked a decent meal and polished off a few of his favorite beers. His headache had started to recede, so now he began to come up with a strategy. He had no idea how he had been able to sense the winning ticket, but he had a strong feeling that he had to keep the party going while he was still hot.

The next day Lenny's head had gone back to the manageable level of pain. To avoid suspicion he went to another variety store a few blocks from his place. This time he took Pop's advice and looked hard at the *Pick 4* tickets, where you could win some real money. The rules said that if you could get the right four numbers you would win $10,000. The tickets cost $2 each, which seemed fair. He picked up a soda and then spent some time staring at the *Pick 4* machine. He didn't know if he would be able to predict a winner here because he couldn't see any tickets. He spent another minute looking at the stack of *Vegas Slotmasters* tickets and didn't see anything at all. He worried that maybe his run of special good fortune was already finished.

"Anything I can help you with, son?" asked the older man sitting behind the counter. He had the usual skeptical stare that most business owners had when someone as ripe and disheveled as Lenny walked into their establishment.

"Uh, I'd like to play the *Pick 4*. I'm feeling pretty lucky today," Lenny answered with his usual grin.

"Sure, kid. You want me to let the machine pick your numbers, or do you have some good ones in mind?"

"Ya know what? I guess I'll pick them myself. Why don't you give me two, please," Lenny replied.

"Here you go, kid. Don't forget me if you win it big, okay? Good luck!" the man said as he handed Lenny the form to fill out his numbers.

Lenny stared at the sheet and tried to concentrate. *Now what?* he asked himself. *Oh well, it was only four bucks*, he thought while trying to calm down, but he knew a lot more than that was riding on these results. He wrote down his birthday numbers on the first line, and suddenly he felt his brain come to life and start to calculate numbers. It reminded him of what it felt like when he struggled back in math class to compute numbers, but it seemed to come from some different place in his head. His brain was cranking through numbers on its own. After a few seconds, the numbers settled on **3628**, and then they began to blink in his mind. Throughout the brief time this process occurred, Lenny's face appeared frozen, as if he were in a trance.

"You okay, kid?" the store owner asked loudly with growing concern. "Hey, you havin' some kinda seizure or sumthin?"

Lenny quickly snapped out of his strange trance, wrote the numbers down on the form, and handed them over. "No worries, sir, I'm doin' fine. Just trying to think of the winning numbers, haha. Keep your fingers crossed for me."

He then paid for his soda and started heading home with his ticket. The owner yelled to him as he left, "Hey, glad you're okay! Made me real nervous for a second there. Thought I was gonna have to call an ambulance or sumthin to pick up your seizurin' ass! Just remember to watch the drawing tomorrow night at eight or check out the paper. Good luck, kid."

Lenny acknowledged the man with a wave and started walking home. He had just rounded the corner from the market when he started to stagger. He fell to his knees from the pain. It felt like a swarm of bees was stinging his head. The sharp pains made it impossible to think or function. All he wanted was to get home and swallow some of his extra-strength aspirin. Before he could take another step, he felt a huge stabbing pain in his head and passed out on the sidewalk.

The next thing Lenny knew he was waking up in the emergency room where he had been about ten days earlier. The same doctor that had helped him before was looking into his eyes with some type of flashlight device. "Mr. Simmons? Lenny? Can you hear me?" he asked with a loud, reassuring voice.

Lenny's voice croaked a bit when he replied, "Ah, yeah, Doc. What happened?" The first thing he noticed was that his headache had receded again to its usual dull throbbing.

"We don't know, Lenny. You were found unconscious

on the sidewalk. We did the usual tests, but we didn't find anything abnormal. You appear to be healing just fine, but this latest incident is worrisome. Can you tell me how you've been feeling since you were in here?" The doctor leaned in with a look of worry and compassion as he listened closely to Lenny's response.

"I don't know what to say, Doc. I've had slight headaches for a while, but the aspirin you gave me kept it pretty well in check. I did feel some kinda pain before I passed out, but otherwise, I've been feelin' pretty good." Lenny gave the Doc his best winning smile and then asked in a more serious tone, "What do you think it could be, Doc? Am I in any danger?"

"Well, it is unusual to lose consciousness like that, but all your tests are normal. You're not even showing the usual symptoms of a slight concussion, which doesn't make sense to me." He frowned slightly, "Are you sure you're telling me everything, Lenny? You haven't been taking any drugs or drinking a lot of alcohol, have you?"

Lenny smiled at the doctor and replied, "Just had a couple beers the other night, Doc. Other than that I can't think of anything unusual to tell you," he lied. "I'm feeling great now."

There was no way Lenny was going to tell the Doc about his newfound ability. For all he knew, they would turn him into a lab rat and study him in a cage with some monkeys in a faraway research center. He was also afraid that whatever medicine they might give him could take his special ability away for good. He wasn't gonna let that happen! He planned on riding his hot streak as long as he could. This was his chance, and nobody was going to take it away from him.

"Okay, Lenny," the doctor replied knowing full well there was more to the story, but also that Lenny wasn't going to tell him about it. "We'll let you sleep here tonight under observation. If you're feeling better tomorrow morning, we'll let you go home. I want to see you back here in a week to check you out again. Just try and get some rest for now." The doctor patted him softly on the shoulder and then left him to sleep.

Lenny slept fine and was feeling reasonably well the next morning. They sent him home with some heavy-duty pain pills and a card reminding him of his appointment the following week.

Lenny spent the next day sleeping in his apartment trying to figure out his next move. He ordered some Chinese food and took some of his pain pills to help him sleep. He still had the dull throbbing in his head, but he hardly even noticed it at this point.

Lenny didn't own a television anymore, so the following morning he jumped out of bed and headed to Pop's Market to buy a newspaper. Pop wasn't in the shop in the early morning but Walt was.

"Hey, there's the lucky man. Up early today. How's life, buddy?" Walt asked with a little more friendliness than usual. "Looking for some more *Vegas Slotmasters* tickets?"

"Ah, not today, Walt. I'll take one of those breakfast burritos and a coffee … oh yeah, and this paper." Lenny acted as if it was the most normal thing in the world to say, but Walt immediately became interested.

"Buying newspapers? Well, now that's interesting, Lenny," Walt said with a smile and continued, "Are you now playing the horses and the stock market, good sir?" He laughed and rang up Lenny's items.

Lenny laughed politely, took his bag of purchases, and quickly walked home. He devoured his burrito, chugged down his coffee, and kept re-reading the newspaper headlines. He read but didn't comprehend whatever they were talking about—some overseas crisis. For some reason, he didn't have the nerve to turn to the section that listed the lottery number winners. He didn't know where this fear was coming from, but he didn't like it. At this point, he wasn't sure if he was more scared about winning than losing.

After about a half hour of procrastinating, Lenny finally turned to the section with the lottery number winners. He looked at the winning numbers and then double-checked the numbers on the ticket in his pocket. The section in the paper reported, *Winning Pick 4 Numbers: 3628*. Lenny's mouth dropped open as he realized there was really something to this thing. He had an unbelievable ability that was going to change his whole life! It had already changed it for the better, and he realized that this was only the beginning.

He took a moment to let it settle in and then smiled broadly. He read the information under the winning numbers that said:

All players with matching Pick 4 numbers, please report to the local lottery headquarters to receive your prize in either check or money order form. Please note that all applicable taxes will be deducted from the final amount.

Lenny looked at the address and noticed that they were open until 5 PM today. He showered and shaved, put on his nicest clothes, and splurged on a cab to get him to the downtown lottery office.

After going through all the formalities at the lottery

office, Lenny walked out with the largest money order he had ever held in his hand. He splurged on another cab ride and set up a checking account at the bank around the corner from his apartment.

Things were moving fast, and he now tried to plan his next moves carefully. There was still nobody that had any idea that any of this was happening, and Lenny wanted to keep it that way. Most importantly, he didn't want to attract any attention. He had heard that people came out of the woodwork if they knew you had won the lottery or come into any money, so he wanted to be cautious. He couldn't resist, however, going to his favorite ribs place that night and ordering whatever he wanted off the menu. What a great feeling it was to have a belly swollen up from overeating. He felt even better when he reminded himself that this was indeed just the beginning.

The next day Lenny had come up with a plan. The money he had won would last him a while, but it wouldn't change his life permanently, and that was what he really wanted. He was nervous, however, about the awful pain that had affected his head after the *Pick 4* scenario. Despite his concern, he felt confident that there was a straightforward way to counteract the pain. The Doc had given him some strong pain pills that he thought would do the trick if he took enough of them at the right moment. Even if they didn't, he figured it was well worth spending some time in the hospital if he could win the *Pick 6* jackpot.

Lenny decided to give his brain a rest for a couple weeks hoping that might help further protect him for his next move. However, he soon began to worry that his special ability could leave at any time. He had been monitoring the *Pick 6* Jackpot in the paper and happily noted that it had grown to more than $200 million. The next drawing was happening the following evening. This was it. He would just have to rest his brain later.

Lenny knew that winning the *Pick 6* jackpot would be an amazing life-changing event, and he smiled thinking of all the incredible things he would do with that fortune. One thing for sure, he wouldn't be spending any more time in this dumpy area. He planned to go far away and see some of the world that he had only dreamed about from reading books and watching TV as a kid. He had always wanted to visit some of the exotic islands in the South Pacific, so he decided he would make Tahiti his new home. All he needed were those *Pick 6* (5 plus one Meteor Ball) numbers, and he would really be all set.

The next morning Lenny strolled confidently to Pop's Market. He had read somewhere that the store that sold winning lottery tickets got a nice cut of the money, so he figured he'd let Pop and Walt get in on some of his action. They had always teased him some, but he knew they liked him deep down. He also wanted to see the looks on their faces when he saw them again as the jackpot winner. He would be taking his official leave as a customer and as a resident of their lousy neighborhood, and he was going to revel in it.

Lenny walked into Pop's with his broad smile and strode right up to the counter with Pop behind it. "I'm taking your advice and going for the *Pick 6*, Pop. Give me three manual tickets, and get ready to be amazed tonight!"

"Good to see you again, Lenny," Pop said with a smirk. "Please don't tell me you're using the last of your winnings to pay for these tickets?"

"I've still got some savings, Pop," Lenny said with his toothy grin. "Dontcha worry about me now!"

Walt chuckled and Pop shook his head with a smile as he handed the form to Lenny to fill in. "Good luck, Lenny. Maybe you can make us all rich this time. I'd be happy even if you only won the $100K prize. No pressure now!"

"Let's see what I can do today then," Lenny chuckled nervously as he began to fill out the first line. He felt a little panicked when he didn't feel anything special working in his brain as he moved onto the next line. He slowly filled out random numbers associated with his address and birthday in the second line. After he finished the second line, he still felt nothing. Now he was really starting to get concerned.

He pleaded inside his head while he waited to write the numbers in the third line, *Please, God, just let me have it long enough for this last one, and then I'm done forever. I promise. Just one more time.*

"C'mon now, Lenny," Walt said, "you're automatically disqualified if you don't fill out your numbers in a timely fashion. The shot clock is about to expire! Haha!"

"Yeah, Lenny," Pop chimed in, "any number is as good as the next. Hurry up, will ya."

Lenny smiled and coolly answered, "You can't hurry greatness, gentlemen. The winners will come to me soon enough."

The father and son looked at each and laughed loudly at his confident response. They then turned to help another customer, who had walked in to get some smokes. Lenny felt like crying. *So much for my life-changing moment*, he said to himself. He felt beyond miserable. He had just started to write in some random numbers when that familiar feeling overtook him again. This time the force came on like a freight train, and he felt like his head was shaking apart as it calculated. The numbers revolved around in his head for about 20 seconds, but it felt like 20 minutes to Lenny. When he finally had the numbers **14 26 33 45 52 11** blinking steadily in his head, he found that he had trouble standing. He leaned against the counter, quickly wrote the numbers in the form, and then handed them to Pop.

Pop eyed him warily as he entered the sets of numbers into the machine and gave Lenny his ticket. "Lenny, what the hell is wrong with you, son? You look like you just woke up from a nightmare. You're sweating like a pig and paler than a ghost. Why don't you just sit down for a minute?" He turned to his son and ordered with some urgency, "Walt, give him that chair, and get the boy some water!"

Walt quickly produced a chair from behind the counter, and Lenny didn't argue as he sat down with a thud. "I just need a minute, thanks," he whispered with an attempt at his winning smile that wasn't cutting it. He sat weakly in the chair for a while, looking like a ventriloquist's dummy not currently in use. He barely moved, breathed deeply and slowly, and had a blank expression on his face.

"Take your time, kid," Pop said with some concern. "Are you going to be alright, or should we call someone? Christ, maybe he's havin' a stroke or sumthin?" he asked Walt helplessly.

After a few scary minutes, Lenny started to come out of his daze and feel somewhat better. Surprisingly, he felt he could at least function now. "I'll be alright, Pop, Walt. Really, no worries now, gentlemen," he said with mock formality as he stood up and began to head to the door. Pop and Walt felt relieved as they noticed that his color was back, and he seemed to at least be able to walk normally.

"You should go home and rest up a bit, Lenny," Pop said with visible relief. He then exhaled, laughed, and said, "Don't worry! We'll let you know if you're the big winner, haha."

Lenny laughed too, waved weakly at both of them and headed home. He had his pain pills with him and planned to use them at the first sign of those awful head pains. He had bought a bottle of water at Pop's to chug the pills down with at the first sign of trouble.

After Lenny walked out, Pop smiled and said to Walt, " 'Fool's gold!' That's what they should really call all these goddamned lottery games. But I guess it's good for the state, and it sure helps our bottom line."

Walt nodded his approval and said, "Yeah, and it also gives people a chance to dream about a better life. That's worth a couple bucks now, isn't it?"

As soon as the stabbing pains began out on the sidewalk, Lenny knew that his pills would not be able to help him. He started swallowing them in large gulps, but it didn't matter. The pain wasn't like a swarm of bees this time; it was more like a room full of angry, venomous snakes that were all clamping their fangs deeply into his head. His brain was on fire. "No!" he cried out in anger and frustration. "This was supposed to be a life-changing event for me! I don't want to be stuck here in this hell anymore! I want to go to Tahiti! I want to be rich and free to do whatever I want! I want t—"

The intensity of the pain somehow increased, and

Lenny's entire body convulsed. He collapsed on the sidewalk, shook a bit more, and was still. A passerby yelled for help, and people started to gather—some to help, but most just to gawk.

Pop and Walt responded quickly to the commotion outside their store. Pop was an Army veteran and had fought in some nasty battles. After taking one look at the unnatural way Lenny was lying on the sidewalk, he knew it was hopeless. He and Walt waited grimly for the paramedics to arrive and make it official. While they waited, Pop noticed that Lenny's *Pick 6* ticket and his receipt had fallen out of his pocket onto the sidewalk next to him. Not really knowing what to do with them, he picked them up and shoved them in his own pocket. He looked down at Lenny's covered-up body and sadly shook his head.

The next day Pop looked at the newspaper and Lenny's *Pick 6* ticket and cried out, "Holy cow! This can't be real." Then he said somberly, "Nobody could be that lucky and unlucky at the same time."

Later in the week, there were two articles of interest in the city's *Daily Gazette*. The first was featured on the front page, and the second appeared on the third page at the bottom of the Metro section.

"Popular Storeowner Wins Lottery Jackpot"

Alonzo "Pop" Martin, the longtime owner of Pop's Market on 316 Spring Street, has claimed the largest jackpot win in the history of our state. Lottery officials confirmed yesterday that Mr. Martin had an exact match of the *Pick Six* lottery numbers including the Meteor Ball, which won him the grand prize of $228 million before taxes.

Mr. Martin and his son, Walt, appeared at a press conference at the lottery office holding a large ceremonial check displaying their massive winning amount. Mr. Martin happily answered reporters' questions at the ceremony, attributing his win to "God's will" and promising that he would immediately be retiring to spend more time with his family.

Mr. Martin also stated that he would be giving a good portion of the winnings to his children. He also plans to make substantial donations to his church and some of his favorite charities. He explained that he felt "it was only right to share the bounty" of his historic win. His son Walt added that his father didn't regularly play the lottery like so many of his customers, but he made a fortunate exception this time because of the enormous size of the *Pick* 6 jackpot.

"Local Man Found Dead of Undisclosed Causes"

Leonard Alden Simmons, 22, of 348 Tomson Blvd was found dead on the sidewalk near the corner of Spring Street and Jefferson Ave on Tuesday morning. Emergency personnel responded to a 911 call at 10:15 AM, but they found Mr. Simmons unresponsive. He was pronounced dead shortly after arrival at Sedgwick General Hospital.

A preliminary police investigation has found no signs of foul play. An autopsy is scheduled later this week to determine the cause of death.

A TREMENDOUS MACHINE

L ars again streamed the video of the 1973 Belmont
Stakes in holograph format. He had found it
during his scheduled rest day while he scrolled
through the many options on his entertainment device.
Lars had grown tired of the usual entertainment sources
and decided to look in some obscure folders he had never
explored. The archival footage of the race was in one of
the historic entertainment folders labeled *Classic Sporting
Events of the 20th Century*.

Lars was again transfixed by the thunderous yelling of
the massive crowd, the galloping of the horses, and the
skilled commentary of the race announcer. The excitement
was overwhelming as he once again experienced what he
had already witnessed at least two dozen times.

The majestic looking horses Secretariat and Sham were
leading the elite field, and then Secretariat began to pull
away decisively. He was increasing his gap steadily on
Sham, and suddenly it was no longer a contested race. It
became only about seeing how fast a wondrous horse

could run. The announcer commented on the dramatic situation with awestruck emotion:

SECRETARIAT IS WIDENING NOW!
HE IS MOVING LIKE A TREMENDOUS MACHINE!
SECRETARIAT BY 12!
SECRETARIAT BY 14 LENGTHS AT THE TURN!

Lars again felt the goose bumps rise up on his arms, and tears came into his eyes. The crowd roared its approval, and the stands shook as Secretariat continued his domination. Even the jockey riding him could not believe the incredible performance and snuck a glance back to see how far behind the rest of the field was.

The crowd and the announcer were mesmerized as Secretariat crossed the finish line 31 lengths ahead in a record-setting time of 2:24 for a mile and a half—a record that Lars read was never broken. The camera panned to Secretariat's owner, and Lars could feel her joy as she celebrated the triumph with her family and friends. Lars smiled as he watched the celebration and felt the energy and happiness radiating throughout the racetrack stands. *To have been there*, he thought wistfully.

In the documentaries about Secretariat's finest performance that Lars had also looked up, he was struck by the powerful emotions that eyewitnesses at the track and those watching around the world felt while watching this impressive performance. For Lars, it was like watching testimony from an alien world.

In his world, living competitors were considered barbaric and one of the many primeval things which his society frowned upon. Human and animal athletes had long ago been replaced by performance droids that were designed and programmed to race, fight, and compete with exact precision. The committees in charge of their respective sporting events discussed and determined the competitive outcomes in a fair and practical manner. Spectators who attended these events watched with the appropriate amount of cheering and behaved properly. Booing, foul language and gestures, object throwing, and other bad behavior were strictly prohibited, and only a moderate amount of gambling was permitted—for bettors who were financially vetted. Virtual viewing of these competitions was encouraged within limits but was prohibited during working hours.

Lars, like everyone else, understood that things were much more civilized now. It made complete sense, of course, to use machines designed for competition that felt no pain and couldn't suffer physically or mentally in sporting events.

Lars smiled again as he reflected on what he had recently learned. He had done some research on horse racing way back in 1973 and found some intriguing nuggets.

He discovered that Secretariat's biggest competitor, Sham, was also quite an impressive horse, who would have won at least the first two legs of the horse racing Triple Crown if Secretariat wasn't around. Sham came in second in both the Kentucky Derby and the Preakness Stakes by just 2 ½ lengths and recorded some of the best times ever in those races. He was also challenging Secretariat in the Belmont Stakes for about half of the race when he sustained a hairline fracture in his right leg. As a result, the jockey eased him back to protect him, and he finished last.

Lars found this information fascinating. However, he also realized that nobody was beating or even challenging Secretariat on that fateful day in 1973, which thrilled him even more.

Lars' entertainment device now asked if he would like to experience the race in virtual reality from Secretariat's point of view. It also offered him the option of riding on one of the other horses or changing the outcome of the race. He had tried these and other simulations earlier, but it just couldn't come close to the experience of watching the real thing. The video holograph format of the race was the best he could do.

Lars sighed as he looked out the tinted windows of his living pod and again ordered up the video holograph of the 1973 Belmont Stakes.

THE RUBBING MAN

Milo Flintock carefully rubbed the sunscreen onto every exposed part of his body as he prepared to venture out into the blazing sunlight. Luckily, he was an exacting person who abhorred wastefulness above almost anything else. He knew that there was only so much sunscreen left in the bottle and that without it things would become quite painful. He made sure he didn't waste a drop.

Flintock had developed a circular rubbing motion that overlapped exposed areas just enough to ensure every bit of skin was covered with the minimal amount of waste. The agony he still felt on a small spot just behind his elbow was a constant reminder that he had to be careful and deliberate in applying the sunscreen. He took his time rubbing the lotion slowly and thoroughly—time was the one thing he had in spades.

Flintock knew exactly how far the fresh water spring was from his residence. He also knew how quickly the unforgiving sun's rays would eat up his carefully applied sunscreen. He had exactly three minutes and thirty-two seconds to run to the spring, fill up his two metal containers, and return safely to his small but sturdy residence. Just to be on the safe side, he would be back within exactly three minutes ten seconds. He definitely didn't want to experience that hellish pain again. God help him if he tripped or injured himself somehow and couldn't get back to his residence in time.

As he carefully rubbed the protective lotion on the back of his neck, Flintock thought back to how he had gotten to this point and calculated again, for at least the hundredth time, what his chances were of being rescued.

#

Flintock had been an Outer Rim Colonist, Class Two-Agricultural Research Specialist, on Planet Limbar Six for the last three Earth years. He and 149 other qualified applicants had been "fortunate" enough to win a lottery to get this coveted assignment. Their mission was to perform agricultural research to determine if Limbar Six would be suitable for long-term agricultural production and possible planetary-level colonization.

Limbar Six had many enviable qualities for agricultural development and colonization. Most importantly, the planet had an atmosphere and climate remarkably like Earth, negating the need for an expensive and confining dome. The planet also had an abundance of fresh water and a colorful variety of flora, but not much fauna. There also weren't any intelligent inhabitants that needed to be dealt with nor any dangerous predatory creatures that might make life unpleasant. There were hordes of nasty cockroach-like insects that eagerly consumed vegetation, but they weren't a safety threat. Flintock's research team had to eliminate these insects from the area, which wasn't difficult using the standard pesticide treatment.

The planet's climate was also extremely calm and pleasant. The preliminary testing done by the Authorities' unmanned probes determined that the temperature never varied more than four degrees Celsius and was always between 26 and 30 degrees in the selected areas for testing and possible colonization. The weather was similar to the tropics on Earth but even milder, as there was sufficient rain but no violent storms. In addition, for reasons that Flintock didn't really understand having to do with its orbit, magnetic field, and other features, some areas of the planet were in perpetual daylight. This phenomenon was similar to the White Nights in Finland and Russia but warmer, brighter, and constant. The Authorities' probes calculated that those regions would stay that way for at least a century. In short, Limbar Six seemed like it would be an ideal place for an agricultural settlement. However, it still required more extensive testing, which would be conducted by five small research stations in different areas of the planet.

Because of the extremely strict weight restrictions for the transfer flight, the research team members had each been ordered to pack only one protective hat and just a few changes of clothing—all designed for tropical weather. As a result, most people only brought one or two long sleeve shirts or pants and one standard set of rain gear. There was also no need to bring towels or linens as their pre-fabricated residences had automated hand and body dryers and the latest in pod sleeping technology.

Since the Authorities had determined there were no

credible threats on Limbar Six, they had deemed it unnecessary to leave any security forces on the planet. They also did not designate any fast response rescue teams for the planet because it was too remote of a sector. Those highly trained and costly resources were reserved for the vast amount of unlucky colonists and research teams living in cramped, domed settlements on lifeless moons and planets. The research stations on Limbar Six were, for the most part, on their own.

Things went well for Flintock and his fellow researchers for more than three years. The team experimented with the crops they brought and discovered some promising new forms of agricultural life. They had been amazed at how fast their crops had grown in the nutrient-rich soil under constant sunlight. The team didn't even need to use any fertilizer to grow the biggest and most vital crops that any of them had ever seen.

One peculiar thing the team members observed was the lack of trees or any larger bushes. Some unknown factor seemed to have prevented larger forms of agriculture from prospering there. That feature was something that would require more investigation.

On the day things turned bad, Flintock was resting in his residence on doctor's orders. The day before he had developed a surprisingly severe infection on top of his right hand that needed treatment. He had been clearing some of the scrub brush near his personal garden when he scratched himself badly on some thorns. Minor first aid didn't heal the wound, and he had developed a strong fever. The settlement doctor prescribed antibiotics, gave him some healing ointment, and told him to rest inside for 48 hours.

Because of his minor illness, Flintock was resting comfortably looking out his residence window when the horrible event occurred. Otherwise, he would have been fried like the rest of them.

The other 29 team members at the station were out in the main farm area, just like any other workday, when it hit. Flintock was no astrophysicist, but his best guess was that it was some type of solar flare or another solar event that had occurred. All that actually mattered was that it did some serious damage.

What Flintock experienced was a brilliant flash of light and a rush of hot air (even in his climate-controlled residence), and then things changed dramatically. He immediately heard some high-pitched screaming in the distance and saw the team members running wildly back toward his residence area. They didn't have a chance.

As far as Flintock could figure out, the solar flare, or whatever it was, had damaged the planet's protective atmosphere. As a result, the sun's powerful rays radiated down to the surface unfiltered and unhindered. Within less than two minutes, the screaming had stopped and the entire research team lay scattered throughout the farm area. The sun's intense rays had hit their poorly protected skin and burned them to death.

Flintock could only remain safely inside and stare helplessly at the horrifying scene and its aftermath.

After a tough day of introspection, Flintock had managed to somewhat get over his shock. Luckily, the antibiotics had worked. His hand was feeling better, his fever had broken, and he had some energy. Flintock then began to formulate and execute a survival plan.

In the two months since the terrible event, he had

considered and tried multiple actions to increase his chances of survival, but most of them had been thwarted by the unforgiving planet and sunlight. Flintock realized he had been fortunate to survive the initial onslaught, but in the days that followed, it seemed that all his luck had disappeared. Everything appeared to be working against him in epic proportions.

First, the solar flare's initial burst had sparked a reaction with some of the chemicals in the roofing material of the residence and ignited a small fire. When Flintock noticed the smoke, he had managed to quickly put out the fire by applying the chemical extinguisher solution through the escape hatch in the ceiling. However, a similar fire destroyed the unprotected supply sheds in his yard. That fire was extremely costly, as his rain gear, a long sleeve shirt and pants, some small tarps, assorted tools and supplies, additional food tablets, and his washing device (holding most of his limited clothing) were all destroyed.

Second, since he preferred to live alone, he had volunteered to take the one residence nearest to the common farm area. This made it easy to get back and forth to work, but the Main Residential Area (MRA) was a good fifteen-minute jog away. Since there was virtually no shade anywhere, he had nowhere to stop and reapply the sunscreen on any long run there looking for supplies.

To make matters worse, Flintock knew that the MRA had also been severely damaged, even if he could manage to get there. On the first day of the event after putting out the fire in his residence, Flintock had noticed huge plumes of black smoke in the distance coming from the MRA. That smoke meant that the structures there were severely damaged, if not completely destroyed.

Third, the solar event had destroyed the technical infrastructure at his residence. The blast had disabled the power and, consequently, his plumbing and all the electronics no longer worked. Having no climate control caused him to sweat more, which meant he required additional water. This was also working against his survival.

When it took out the power, the solar flare also wiped out the communications system, so Flintock was unable to send any distress signals. In addition, even if he could manage to send a signal, he estimated it would take at least 60-90 days for the Authorities to organize a rescue expedition and get to this remote location.

Fourth, the two solar-powered rovers the team members used to quickly shuttle back and forth from the MRA to the farm area were both overloaded and disabled by the solar blast. Flintock learned this unhappy fact on a costly run to the edge of the farm area—where they were normally parked during the workday.

Since he couldn't run there, he had planned to use one of the rovers to drive to what was left of the MRA to try to find more clothes for cover along with additional supplies. Instead, he used up some of his valuable sunscreen just to get there and back and gained nothing. Flintock was lucky that there was just enough room to crawl under one of the rovers. He took his time and carefully used its shade to let him apply his sunscreen for the run back to his residence.

With no rover transportation and without any possibility of shade during the long run to the MRA, there was no way for Flintock to get there safely. As a result, any already slim hopes of recovering extra clothes, supplies, and maybe even someone else's extra-strength bottle of sunscreen were lost.

Fifth, his idea to salvage the clothes and supplies from the bodies lying in the farm area didn't work because the nasty cockroach insects had returned in droves. These pests were impervious to the intense sunlight and actually seemed energized by the new environment. They were busily consuming all the dead crops in the farm area, along with a decent amount of the natural vegetation that had been cooked by the sunlight. Some smaller types of scrub bush seemed unaffected by the intense sunlight, but the cockroaches left them alone. In addition to vegetation, the insects consumed all the clothing on the team members' burnt bodies.

Flintock felt nauseated when he noticed that the skin on the bodies had first turned black and then had melted away completely. The only thing remaining at this point were sun-bleached bones and some metal water bottles and agricultural tools. He hadn't been friends with any of the other team members, but it saddened him when he thought of the pain and fear they experienced in their last moments. Nobody deserved such an awful end.

Luckily, the disgusting insects had plenty of food to eat in the farmed areas and wild fields all around him. They didn't seem interested in his boxy residence made out of metal and other synthetic materials—at least not yet.

Finally, there was another glaring problem: he didn't have enough extra-strength sunscreen to last indefinitely waiting for rescue. All team members had been allotted a decent amount of standard sunscreen, which worked fine in the normal climate. However, it only lasted about 30 seconds in the new situation. Flintock had learned that disturbing fact when he tested this sunscreen right near the beginning of the whole mess. He had carefully applied it to the top of his left hand and stuck it out of one of his residence's small windows into the direct sunlight. After 30 seconds of exposure, he had felt the heat building up to the point of burning.

Aside from his initial survival and shelter, his bottle of extra-strength sunscreen was the major positive factor Flintock could appreciate. However, having that bottle was really a result of Flintock's thorough planning as opposed to luck.

Since Flintock had a fair complexion, he had used some of his limited transport weight allotment to bring in a good-sized bottle of extra-strength sunscreen. The well-known brand he brought was supposed to be six times stronger than normal sunscreen. He didn't think he was going to have to use it that much, but he wanted to have it around if the weather changed or if he spent longer in the sun than he anticipated. He never dreamed that it would ultimately save his life.

Flintock tried the same hand test with his extra-strength sunscreen and found that it actually *was* six times more powerful than the normal brand. He was ecstatic that, for once, there was truth in advertising!

Unlike most people facing difficult situations, Flintock didn't waste much time despairing, but he instead continued to do what he did best: plan, experiment, and execute. He had carefully proceeded to take stock of his situation after his initial setbacks.

Flintock knew the other research stations were too far away to reach, especially under the planet's current conditions. He had to assume they were all gone, too.

Flintock determined that his best hope was that the Authorities would stop by on one of their intermittent official status check-ins to monitor the mission progress and, more importantly for them, obtain crop samples for research and distribution. He knew that the average colony or research station check-in time was between three to four years, so he felt he was already somewhere near that timeframe. The key to his survival was to stretch out his provisions and the sunscreen long enough until the Authorities returned.

On the positive side, he had the residence to shelter him and keep him alive, along with a good supply of food tablets and dried up crops in his pantry. He also had the clothes on his back, one spare outfit, his hat, his sunglasses, and his sunscreen to protect him from the sunlight. He was also lucky to have the spring so close.

In addition to all the initial setbacks, there were other negative factors to overcome. The spring did provide him with his required water; however, he had to run there every few days to fill up his containers. That necessary run meant he had to go outside under the sun's now dangerous rays and use his sunscreen. He was also going through his supply of food a little quicker than he first thought, so he had started to ration it accordingly. That resource was unreplaceable, just like the sunscreen. He planned, therefore, to trade a little more hunger for extra time as was required. He believed that he could stretch out the food tablets until his ultimate rescue, but he planned to be more drastic with the rationing in the near future. He wanted to be prepared if necessary, even though he remained confident the check-in would occur well before things got uncomfortable.

Flintock was meticulous and had plenty of time to experiment, so he exhausted every option he could think of to increase his odds of survival. For example, he tried to use some pieces of metal he removed from inside the residence as cover. Unfortunately, the sunlight quickly made the metal objects too hot to wear. The material on the roof was the only thing that stopped the powerful rays, and it was impossible to break off without heavy tools.

He also realized the value of his one extra set of clothing, which he kept in reserve, because his clothing, hat, and boots would always deteriorate a little after each trip to the spring. He calculated how long it took for a hole to form in the fabric of these items and set aside a pile of ripped up reserve clothing patches to cover these gaps. Flintock was confident that with this method he could extend his limited amount of clothing for a sufficient amount of time, but he had to closely monitor the surface areas of his clothes, hat, and boots.

In addition, he tried hard to find a substitute or enhancement for his extra-strength sunscreen. He tested some of the soil as mud caked on his skin and tried it in combination with lesser amounts of standard and extra-strength sunscreen. His hand tests quickly revealed that nothing even came close to the magical three minutes and twenty-two seconds protection he already had, via his patented rubbing in of the extra-strength sunscreen. He found ways to get the other combinations up to about 45 seconds, but he had to continuously reapply the mud-sunscreen mixture after that point. The painful rays hitting his exposed body areas would have made that impossible to do without shelter. The spring was too far away for these crude methods to be of much help.

In his most recent experiments, Flintock thought he might be able to provide even more protection by adding some of the synthetic contents from a couple of bottles of *Morale Boost*. He had brought along this coveted mental refreshment in the hopes of celebrating some special occasions. Luckily, there hadn't been any significant celebrations during the mission, so he had nearly two full bottles to work with in his experiments.

#

Flintock now focused on the present as he prepared for his next run to get water from the spring. He had the rubbing process down to an exact science and was confident in his preparations. He had also figured out the maximum amount of time he should wait to get new water and, consequently, expend his precious sunscreen.

With his strict attention to detail, he again thought that he might really have a chance. Flintock tried hard to remember if the usual check-in time was closer to three years or four years. He wasn't sure if there was a difference between check-in times for research stations vs. colonies. Even if the time was closer to four years, he assured himself that he could still make it with the proper planning and execution.

As Flintock was finishing up his current rubbing process, he drifted back to his school days. He had always been fascinated with plants and soil, so he had naturally studied agronomy at the state learning center. His school friends frequently teased him because they so often found him experimenting with different types of soil. He also always seemed to have dirty hands and soil smeared on his face during his intense studies. His nickname became

"Muddy Milo," and he actually didn't mind it.

What would they call me now? he thought as he looked down at the drops of sunscreen on his hands. He laughed and recited a customized first verse of an ancient nursery rhyme he remembered, "Rub-a-dub-dub, one man wishes he had a tub!" *Full of sunscreen*, he continued in his head even though it didn't rhyme, and then he smiled.

After he recited the nursery rhyme again, his new nickname suddenly came to him with astonishing clarity: *The Rubbing Man.*

Flintock thought about how fitting the name was because his skills in rubbing the sunscreen evenly and stretching it out as much as possible were keeping him alive. He kept smiling as he finished up the rubbing process.

"Why not?" he said aloud. "I actually kind of like it."

#

After his latest run to the spring, Flintock sat on the metal chair built into his small kitchen and sipped the delicious water. He closed his eyes and tried to calm down. The last trip had been successful, but it had also been more eventful than normal.

Flintock had run to the spring and began filling up his first large container as usual. After about thirty seconds, he felt a strange burning sensation on the top of his right foot. When he glanced down, he was startled to see about two dozen of the cockroach-like insects calmly sitting on the boot covering his right foot. They were chewing away on the boot in a determined rhythm. He shook his boot violently, but the insects stubbornly remained. Flintock then angrily brushed the little bastards off with disgust using his free hand. However, although the bugs were quickly dispersed, the burning feeling intensified. He looked down again and noticed with horror that the little team of insects had managed to chew multiple small holes through the tongue on the top of the boot and the sunlight was now burning his exposed right foot. He always went sockless in his boots because his only three pairs of socks had been destroyed along with the washing device in the supply shed. The boots used to provide enough cover.

Flintock tried to remain calm and keep track of the elapsed time as usual—otherwise, he would have bigger problems than a burnt foot. He still had two minutes and fifteen seconds left, and he knew that it would take precisely one minute and three seconds to run back to the safety of the residence. He spent a precious few seconds rubbing the recent build-up of sweat off his hands.

Flintock then reached into the right front pocket of his shorts and took out the small bottle he had filled with extra-strength sunscreen in case of emergency. The pain in his foot had become excruciating, but he carefully unscrewed the top and poured just enough sunscreen into his hand to protect the top of his exposed foot. He quickly performed his special rubbing motion, as he didn't want to waste a drop. His foot still hurt, but he could tell that the intense rays were now being blocked. He hurriedly filled up as much as he could of the second water container and ran for home before it was too late.

The next day Flintock rubbed more healing ointment onto the top of his aching foot, ate some food tablets, drank a small ration of water, and pulled out his marker to record the day's experiments. He wrote down his findings on the residence wall next to the kitchen. This area now contained his exhaustive notes on a large variety of potentially protective solutions for his exposed skin. He wrote in his own personal shorthand to preserve as much space as possible. The residence still had a decent amount of untouched wall space, but he always liked to plan ahead. He then inspected his clothes and hat and marked the growing amount of worn and fraying areas where patching would be needed before the next run.

As he looked out the residence window, Flintock noticed that some of the cockroach-like insects had now invaded his personal garden and were feasting there. They were definitely getting closer on all sides, but he felt secure that they still had plenty of other things to eat. Their increased presence near the spring was definitely alarming, and he now would have to pay careful attention while he filled up his containers. That new burden would cost him time, which would cost him water, and ultimately would cost him sunscreen and protection as well.

Unfortunately, the pesticide had been stored in one of his sheds and back at the MRA, so those little bastards were here to stay. Flintock also wondered how effective the usual treatment would have been against them in their newly energized state—maybe it would now take extra-strength pesticide to get rid of them? He also noted that he would now have to rub in a little more sunscreen to protect the small area that the boot no longer covered—or he could try to patch the holes. These were just more complications that he would have to overcome.

Flintock clenched his teeth as his burnt foot began to act up a bit despite the ointment. Now he had that small area of seared flesh, along with the spot under his elbow, to remind him to be thorough with the rubbing process.

He also realized that if it ultimately came to it, he would have to sacrifice some small regions of his exposed skin to make the necessary run to the spring. He wouldn't be at that point in the near future, but he assured himself that he would make the necessary calculations to determine how to extend those life-giving runs. He would carefully assess which parts of his exposed body would be able to take the burning yet still allow him to run fast enough to complete his mission. He hoped it would never come to that, but he would be prepared as always.

His stomach gurgled softly, and he tried to rub the hunger pains away. He thought he had rationed the calories correctly to avoid this level of hunger, but he must not have accounted for everything. Flintock speculated that the more intense exertion on this latest run had likely resulted in the loss of more electrolytes and burned more calories. He made a note that he would also have to account for the loss of more calories in the next phase. This would definitely become a factor when some sections of the body would be exposed and stressed during the run.

He tried to ignore any more thoughts on these unpleasant topics. It was now time to focus his attention on his important experiments.

Flintock took a few moments to reassure himself that his carefully planned and well-executed efforts were going to work in the end. He knew that it was now more than three years and two months since the research mission began. He continued to feel confident that the Authorities check-in time was coming ever nearer.

The rubbing man exhaled deeply, gathered up his various materials, and got to work preparing for the day's scheduled hand tests.

ALL HAIL CAESAR!

Julius Caesar was looking exceptionally pale this morning, and his mouth was gasping a bit for air. He was currently lying with a slight tilt between the sunken pirate ship and a hollowed-out wooden log in Barnaby's 50-gallon aquarium. Barnaby was afraid he might have to move the beautiful Opaline Gourami to his hospital tank, but he would make that decision after school. He couldn't wait to get the boring school day over and be back here to continue his ongoing battles.

Barnaby spotted the Zebra Danios darting around and solemnly ordered, "Praetorian Guard, do what you must to protect your leader until our next great battle." He put his hand on the side of the aquarium and interpreted the quick reversal in their swimming motion as a signal that his orders were understood. "All hail Caesar!" he said loudly as he copied the Roman salute he had seen in his history book. Then he turned off the aquarium hood light (to prevent any algae blooms) and ran upstairs and outside to catch the school bus.

After another long day at school, except of course during Ancient History and Creative Writing, Barnaby was back in command of his troops. He had brought along his friend, Arthur, as a trusted advisor. Julius Caesar had thankfully recovered from his temporary ailment and was swimming regally around the tank. Today Barnaby was reenacting the Battle of Alesia, one of Caesar's greatest triumphs in the Gallic Wars.

"Ya see, Artie, look at all those Tiger Barbs swimming around. Those little guys represent the Gallic forces, which outnumbered the Roman forces four to one." Arthur looked on agreeably nodding his head and carefully listening to Barnaby. "Now you see how the Black Tetras aren't as many, but they swim more powerfully and push right past the Barbs whenever they feel like it? Well, that represents how much better organized the Roman Legions were and the superior infantry tactics they used. They always were equipped with better weapons and armor and protected themselves with their testudo formation. They also had this awesome cavalry that they used to outflank their enemies."

"That's epic stuff," Arthur commented quietly.

Before Arthur could ask any questions Barnaby continued, "The Romans were also the best at siege warfare, which is what this battle was about. The Romans had all kinds of artillery devices they used to bombard their enemies and weaken their fortresses. This was way before gunpowder and cannons, too. They had things called *Tormenta* that would shoot different projectiles, including flaming javelins! And they also used these devices called *Ballistas*, which were like giant crossbows that shot huge projectiles and rocks at an enemy. Scary stuff when you think of it! Imagine being in some castle or in the forest being shot at by those things!"

"Barn, did Caesar and the Romans ever lose a battle?" Arthur asked as he watched the fish and imagined the ancient battle.

"Well, I read once that they had a tough time invading Britain," Barnaby replied with squinting eyes while he tried to recall what he had read. "But, I don't think he ever technically lost a battle. However, I also read that he always felt inferior compared to the accomplishments of Alexander the Great. He conquered far more territory than Caesar did before he died at age 32."

"That's really cool, Barn," Arthur said genuinely. "Hey, wanna go play some COD? I feel like kicking your butt! Or we can go multiplayer if you feel like beating up on some fresh meat."

Barnaby agreed with a smile, and the boys headed upstairs to play video games.

Barnaby's parents were in the kitchen. They saw the boys heading for the family room, and his mom called out, "Barn, remember that dinner is in an hour, so don't get too hooked on your game."

"Yes, Mom," Barnaby said with slight embarrassment. "All we need to do is pause it anyway."

"You know that Artie is always welcome to stay for dinner. Tacos tonight!"

"Okay, Mom," Barnaby replied dutifully with his response muffled as he closed the door to the family room.

Barnaby's dad smiled saying, "Well, at least he got Artie down to the battlefield for a little bit before the video games won out!"

"Artie's a good kid with a great imagination, too. They're probably the only 11-year-olds in this entire town not sitting around hypnotized like zombies in front of their phones."

As if on cue, Barnaby's older sister Gwen walked by texting on her phone, earbuds firmly in place.

"Don't walk into the wall, honey," her dad jokingly said as she passed by them without a second glance.

He turned back to his wife with a sly grin and continued, "I just can't wait for another Barnaby parent-teacher meeting for some more entertainment! I've never seen a history teacher so exasperated."

"Hey, come on now. Barn didn't mean to correct him in front of the whole class. When he learns something he remembers it, and woe be to those who don't know their facts!"

"My all-time favorite line though is from his English teacher about his creative writing: 'The boy is talented, but I wonder sometimes where he gets his ideas for those stories. Some of them are so dark—and at his age!' " He chuckled and continued, "I wanted to tell her that I personally make him watch all the best scary and intriguing late night fare, but it just ain't true. The boy reads and watches things, remembers everything, and comes up with different takes on it all. Don't ask me why or how!" He looked at his wife with an interesting combination of pride and bewilderment.

"Things could be so much worse!" Barnaby's mother answered. "The guidance counselor just advised that we keep his intellect focused, and he could really achieve some great things," she smiled proudly and hopefully. "And, you know, he is really growing up. He's gotten so much better with taking care of his fish and actually puts away all his plastic soldiers now."

"He's got troops everywhere, and they're all ready for old or new battles depending on the day!"

"Hey, remember when he didn't change the filter cartridge, or do enough water changes for that aquarium? Ugh!" the mom said with a wince. "Thank God, there are no more late night requests for help unclogging the filter or fishing out one of his dead soldiers. His fish are definitely lasting a lot longer now. I think he really is ready for that saltwater tank he wants."

"Smooth sailing ahead, captain!" the dad said as he playfully took her hand. "Hey, really looking forward to those tacos. Make sure you make a couple extra for one of Barnaby's favorite commanding officers, okay?"

The next day after school Barnaby was back alone staring at his fish tank. He felt it was time to move onto new battlefields because he had pretty much exhausted Caesar's campaigns. He consulted his trusted elders, a Ghost Shrimp that had somehow survived for weeks in his tank despite its small size, and a Striped Raphael Catfish that spent most of his time holed up in the hollowed-out log. He called them Cicero and Cato, respectively, after the famed wise senators of Caesar's time.

His first thought was to go back in time and fight some of the epic battles of the Punic Wars. His Australian Rainbow Tetra would make a great Hannibal! He also thought that maybe he had been on to something earlier with Artie and that it was time to explore a new civilization and its legendary military leader. Alexander the Great's campaigns were awe-inspiring, and he had only just begun to learn about them.

Having a saltwater tank would also allow him to bring all kinds of new and colorful creatures into his recreated battles. His mind whirred as he thought of all the exotic peoples Alexander and his men had encountered—Barnaby had learned in class that they had campaigned for more than ten years all the way to India! However, he didn't know when his parents would let him take the big step of moving up to a saltwater tank.

As his brain worked, an image suddenly popped into his head of the Battle of Thermopylae between the Greek City States (led by the vastly outnumbered Spartans) and the mighty Persian Empire. The Opaline Gourami would work well as the Spartan leader Leonidas, but he wasn't sure which of his fish he could use to represent the Persian Emperor Xerxes I and his massive army.

Barnaby made a mental note to ask his mom about a trip to the pet store in the near future. He still had enough room for a few new fish, but he always made sure to heed the strict rule of one inch of fish per one gallon of water. He also constantly monitored the temperature, PH, and ammonia levels in the tank. In addition, he did regular water changes, replaced the filter cartridges as necessary, and periodically used a siphon vacuum to clean the gravel well. Barnaby also treated his fish to a wide variety of fish food and treats because nothing was too good for his troops! Somewhere he had read "an army marches on its stomach." He thought maybe Napoleon had said that, but he would have to look that quote up again.

Barnaby figured that an African Leaf Fish would work for Xerxes I, and a small school of Neon Tetras could represent the Persian hordes. He needed to check with the pet store if those types of fish would be compatible in his community tank. If not, he thought a Silver Dollar could also work well for Xerxes I.

He opened the lid of the aquarium and sprinkled some bloodworms on the water surface to spark some activity in the tank. The fish excitedly darted around enjoying their tasty treat. Barnaby smiled broadly as he said out loud to his faithful troops, "The possibilities are endless!"

NIGHT CLOUDS

YET ANOTHER NICE MESS

Astronaut Martin Newell
Personal Log Transcription
Space Station *Lincoln One*

Stanley is driving me crazy today, playing incessantly with the control panel that monitors the oxygen level in the station. Even weightlessness doesn't deter him from getting his paws on those inviting black knobs. Luckily, any cabin adjustments need to be entered in twice with a command prompt, which I don't think Stanley knows. He's definitely a bit of a pain but still good company, especially in light of what's happening down below. I'll take a cat over fanatical humans any day. The worst cats can do is scratch or bite you or maybe infest you with fleas—problems that you can usually solve pretty easily. They won't be solving the problems down there anytime soon.

Stanley has now bitten a slight hole in one of the plastic

hoses behind my seat, and it has gotten loose and started to flail around a bit.

"Well, thanks for yet another nice mess, Stanley," I say to him with a dramatic flourish knowing that it's really only a quick fix. I'm also secretly happy that I have something to do, no matter how mundane, to distract me a little bit from the events happening below.

Gently scolding Stanley with a comment inspired by the famous Oliver Hardy phrase (more on that later) brings back the memories of how this current mission came to be. I've got a relatively free next couple of hours assignment-wise as this is a scheduled rest day, so I might as well record some things for myself and posterity in this trusty personal journal. Command is always pestering me to provide more biographical notes for the reporters on the space beat, so maybe some of these recollections and observations will answer a few questions.

I've also thought about writing a book of my experiences to sell when I'm back on Earth in my retirement, so I might as well keep this journal updated with what I've been up to in orbit. How I got up here is also an interesting story that's worth telling. I can likely use both types of content for my book, so why not record it? One thing I've never had a problem with is talking about myself, so here goes.

In short, when I reflect on my life I can say that everything has really come together almost perfectly for me after beginning rather badly. I've come one hell of a long way from the young kid raised in a broken home. That unpleasant kid was perpetually angry at his absent father and the world.

To her credit, my mother was around somewhat and

tried to love and support me, but there was no real understanding between us. My father's infrequent visits left me distrusting and angry, but it also forged a burning desire in me to prove myself a success without his love and support.

I can thank my parents for giving me exceptional genes resulting in a superior IQ, incredible physical stamina, and great athletic ability, but their lousy parenting pushed me toward being a loner.

In my youth, I sought refuge in the things that fascinated me and came easily, including science and math. I also excelled at sports and focused on football as the most logical way to secure a full scholarship to a prestigious university. At the same time, my rebellious side pushed me toward fabricating a variety of chemical concoctions that other kids paid a small fortune to get. I bankrolled that easy money but quickly stopped this risky activity once I got my football scholarship to State.

I've always happily been a classic loner in every sense with one exception. Outside of my scientific curiosity to raise frogs, salamanders, fruit flies, and other creatures for experiments, I had never had any real interest in pets. I think my parents succeeded in making me doubt love and loyalty from any source. This changed abruptly, though, when I was coming home from the Chemistry lab one night, and I heard a pitiful meowing in an alleyway.

I normally would have just ignored this strange sound as I wanted to get home, and the rain was soaking me right through my cheap windbreaker. However, there was something so desperate and yet still a little defiant about the cry that it intrigued me enough to investigate further. When I shined my phone flashlight into the alleyway, I saw the most pathetic, yet lovable face I have ever witnessed. It was a black and white tuxedo kitten, probably about three months old. His fur was drenched, and he was trying desperately to hide underneath the garbage dumpster where some semi-dry crumpled newspapers lay. I kneeled down and called softly to him, "Hey, buddy. Come over here, little guy. I'll take you home and get you dry. I've even got some tuna fish there that you can have." I never really liked the stuff anyway.

To my surprise, the kitten came out from under the dumpster and slowly but surely walked to me. He eyed me nervously, but I think he realized he was at the point where he would have to take a chance. The first thing he did when he reached me was rub himself against my legs and purr a little as he looked up with hopeful eyes. That precious face and his affection cinched the deal for me. I took my windbreaker off, picked him up carefully, and wrapped him as warmly and tightly as I could in my arms. I walked briskly back to my place and gave him as much tuna as I thought his poor little stomach could take.

Soon Tennessee and I were inseparable. God, how I loved that cat, and how he loved and understood me. He intuitively knew when I was looking for some comforting and when I wanted to focus on something alone. He was the perfect companion for me. He stayed with me all through school and through my first positions at a well-known aerospace company. He was even still around when I was accepted to the astronaut training program and began the arduous process to travel to the heavens.

When I finally lost Tennessee during my time at training, I wept for days and actually took the only personal days off of my career. The only thing that broke my true misery after some time was a trip to the local shelter. I picked up a gray tabby kitten I named Stanley there. When I first met him, he reminded me a lot of Tennessee with maybe even a little more playfulness, and he seemed the most eager to go with me.

Stanley is now nuzzling me in the armpit area while I do my required daily instrument check. He does this periodically as if he were still a little kitten, but it doesn't bother me. He doesn't seem to mind that my undershirt is a little gamey as he stretches out his claws and purrs loudly.

Since we've finished all of our unscheduled work, I've decided to relax by watching our favorite classic comedy duo, Laurel and Hardy. I discovered them as a child one lonely Saturday morning when I was forced, as usual, to provide my own entertainment. Their slapstick routines and witty comments instantly changed my mood, and I found myself laughing uncontrollably—believe me that's a rare occurrence. I always watch them when I need some de-stressing and a good laugh.

Right after I got Stanley, I noticed his rapt attention whenever I had them up on screen. He seemed to be following their routines along with me. I quickly named him Stanley because his personality was more in-tune with Stan Laurel than Oliver Hardy. Since he's always getting into trouble, I frequently use lines similar to Hardy's famous catchphrase as a way of lovingly scolding him.

I just heard on the radio from one of my few companions up here in the dark void, Cosmonaut Valentin Masarov. He's been up here even longer than me because those Russians are extremely tight with their exploration budget. He's been alone, too, for the past few months since they recalled Yuri—again for budgetary reasons I think. He started right off teasing me with his deep voice and ridiculously strong Slavic accent saying, "Hey, Martin, what do you think of my latest move? I think this might put me up by a couple games in our never-ending chess match."

I responded with the proper cockiness saying, "Valentin, let's not get too confident. Remember how nobody thought that clunky computer Big Blue could beat Kasparov way back when? Now it's laughable to think your compatriot actually had a chance. I've got a few surprises I've been waiting to spring on you that might help me pull it out yet. I was captain of the chess club at State you know!"

It was a pleasant enough conversation, but then Valentin's voice and mood had darkened dramatically. His normally booming voice had become little more than a whisper as he said, "My good friend, it looks like our countries are getting to that point of no return, ay? My commander just told me not to expect any resupply for at least another month. They're deploying all available resources to the Situation Zone, and space operations are an even lower priority now. I barely have enough to survive until then." He paused for a second then continued, "We don't have the advanced nutrient technology capsules and water converters that you spoiled Yanks have. I'm keeping the fingers crossed for us and for them. God watch over us, my friend."

"C'mon Valentin, our leaders can't possibly be that stupid, can they?" I had asked with more doubt than I revealed. "It's just a juvenile game of chicken, the way I see it. Nobody is going to win anything from fighting over that godforsaken zone. Hell, the people who live in that shithole never seemed to want it that much in the first place." I waited for his response, but nothing came, so I kept trying, "We can't possibly go back to another world war—it's just too primitive. We're not fucking chimps pounding on our chests, are we? They'll come to their senses and start focusing on things that are important for the future of the human race, uh … like our missions up here. No worries, comrade."

Valentin hadn't seem convinced, but he finally responded weakly with some hope saying, "May God make it so, my friend. If things get worse down there … we will soon be the last thoughts on anyone's mind." There was a long silence as neither of us had a response to that unnerving thought. He finally continued in a more upbeat voice saying, "Okay, I will check in with you tomorrow after I analyze your pitiful excuse for a defense. Sleep well, and give some big pats to that mangy cat of yours."

I responded to him with a little forced bravado, "Will do, my Russian rebel. *Do svidaniya!*"

Now that the brief crackle of communication has ended, I am startled by how quiet it has become, and how instantly alone I feel. I just ordered Stanley to get over here with some loud kitty calls and whistles. He has quickly squirmed and floated his way over to me. It's funny and impressive how rapidly most humans and animals adapt to moving in weightlessness! Now I am hugging Stanley tightly and scratching him under his chin. He likes the attention and so do I.

Valentin is right about my plush digs. I definitely have a much better living situation than he does in his beat-up relic. Let me give you some interesting information on that score.

Space Station *Lincoln One* is at least four times bigger than where Valentin lives. It was originally designed to house three astronauts and equipped with all the food and water supplies necessary for a five-year mission.

I've also got a lot more room I can use whenever I need or want it thanks to my Spooner Attached Inflatable Space Habitat or SAISH. It's made out of an ultra-thin, but incredibly strong polymer that looks and feels like canvas. This baby expands to about six times the size of the entire station and is adaptable to all types of work or recreation scenarios. It looks like an oval-shaped hot-air balloon when it's fully inflated. Spooner, or whoever designed it, was a genius because it provides a lot of extra space on demand and is easily stowed away when it's not needed. I've only deployed it a couple times, mostly for test purposes, and it was a welcome new look and feel. Stanley and I definitely enjoyed the extra space, which is always at a premium up here.

With only Stanley and me on *Lincoln One*, I estimate we could last about 15 years on our current supplies. The most important developments that made this possible are what Valentin mentioned during our chat.

In the last few years, some other brilliant researchers managed to develop nutrient pills that could each supply a human being with the equivalent of 3,000 calories. Those calories are enough to keep a normal human operating at near peak condition. Amazingly, they have no known side effects and are so efficient that the digestive system processes them through the body with almost no waste. As a result, I normally only have one small bowel movement a month. Let me tell you, the more of those you can avoid up here the better. The little waste I do generate is nutrient rich and used as part of a liquid fertilizer in the hydroponic garden, which takes up one small room of the station. That garden provides some leafy greens and other vegetables that help my digestive system and give me a little dining variety. The pills have different flavors, but they still get dull quickly. The plants also help keep the air even cleaner in the capsule.

To top it all off, I also have a urinary osmosis system that converts 99% of my urine back into drinkable water for use by Stanley, the plants, and me. We also have another system that collects humidity from the air, which provides even more recycled water. With the large storage bays of water on *Lincoln One*, it will be decades before we drink the last drop.

All these systems have been developed for one main reason: to make long-distance space exploration a real possibility. We already had the rocket and transportation technology, but we needed some time to catch up on the technology to make it possible for humans to survive and thrive for many years away from the Earth. Even though there have been some advances in cryogenic technology, it is still very far from being usable for our planned long-distance missions.

We also needed to explore the physical and psychological effects on human beings when they are cooped up in a confined space for a long time. Because of my preferred solitary nature (As you might have guessed, I scored off the charts on the psych test for solo living.), I was quickly recruited to test out these effects. First, they placed me in a mock-up space station at a remote mountaintop location on Earth and then in orbit on this marvel of engineering.

The next exploratory phase is supposed to begin in two years with a trip to Mars, and another mission is planned to Jupiter's largest moon, Ganymede. Probes to both bodies have revealed the crucial presence of considerable ice under their surfaces. The presence of water will allow us to establish real human colonies and begin a new era of space exploration. These new outposts and those that follow will also help ensure the continued existence of our species—no matter what happens on Earth in the future. In these next exploratory phases, we want to avoid the mistakes made with the robotic mining of the moon, which has caused so much conflict and tension.

A married couple is supposed to go on the next mission after Stanley and I work out some of the long-term space travel bugs on *Lincoln One*. For their sake, I hope they get along as well as we do. The nearest marriage counselor is going to be a long ways away.

You've probably been wondering why Stanley is up here with me. Well, the main reason is that I insisted that I wouldn't do the mission without him. There was a huge kerfuffle from the bigwigs about additional costs and potential delays. Most of the extra cost was because they had to re-design some of the nutrient pills to work with Stanley, and they also had to design a waste system that he could use successfully. In the end, the price was insignificant compared to keeping their star astronaut guinea pig on mission. I told them frankly that I enjoy being a loner, but I need my loyal cat companion to be there with me to keep me sane and focused.

The bigwigs reluctantly approved it after much debate.

Some scientists even started to support the addition of a pet companion for the mission regardless of my feelings. They saw it as another interesting wrinkle in the testing of how we humans will function and cope living in a cramped home in the cold emptiness of outer space. For all I know, they'll probably give Stanley some interesting psychological tests when we return, too.

I heard that some of the people at Command make fun of me and call me "Pussy Man" behind my back. Hysterical, huh? I could care less as long as I get to keep my space cat up here with me. The powers that be did reject my request to have some live mice onboard to keep Stanley sharp. Probably for the best, as who knows what would have happened had they started breeding and infested the place. Floating little mouse turds throughout the cabin would have been a bit much as well.

The science whizzes have also engineered the station to spin a certain way that allows for a 9-hour period of artificial gravity. The station does a good job of imitating the feel of Earth gravity, but it's not quite as good as the real thing. I have selected the spin cycle to mimic a working day on Earth from 8 AM to 5 PM. After that, we work in weightlessness for a while, and then I strap me and Stanley in for some entertainment. We do occasionally slip out of our tethers to break the monotony.

After our entertainment time, we move into the sleep module, strap ourselves in to count some sheep, and then begin the whole process over again the next morning. The artificial gravity also allows me to use a variety of exercise equipment to fight against the muscle atrophy caused by weightlessness. After I wake up and have a breakfast snack, I usually do a one-hour exercise routine to get my blood going and strengthen my muscles.

This station also comes equipped with an amazing entertainment and information system that digitally stores all of my favorite books, music, movies, and television shows, as well as any scientific data or other pieces of knowledge I feel like perusing at a particular moment. I've got years to explore this set-up when I'm off-duty, and I've already been quite pleased with what it can do. I'm about halfway through the Laurel and Hardy collection and enjoying every second of it. The one piece of entertainment I avoid on purpose is any sci-fi stuff, as the last thing I want to think about when I'm relaxing is anything to do with space. I used to be a huge *Star Trek*, *Star Wars*, *Celestial Gaps*, and *Rogue Galaxy* fan, but I'll start watching them again when I'm back on Earth in my retirement.

Lincoln One is also equipped with the most advanced telescope I've ever seen or operated. I've been using its sophisticated camera function to take pictures and videos of orbiting satellites and spaceships, such as Valentin's antiquated one. I also occasionally point it out to the stars when Command has a request. We've got dedicated telescopes on plenty of satellites up here already, but sometimes they need me to perform a quick observatory task. One of the best parts of having this camera is that I can zoom it down to Earth and check out geographic features and human structures with ease. Sometimes when I get homesick, I find myself focusing on the Empire State Building, the Grand Canyon, or even my old house near the Cape.

I've decided to take a look at the Situation Zone today to see if anything new is happening. Command hasn't been talking too much to me lately. I think everyone is preoccupied with what's going on in the zone. It is definitely disturbing to see the continued massing of mega-drones and armored vehicles, both manned and unmanned, all around the border down there.

I'm now adjusting the camera to be sure of what I think I'm observing in the area. It looks like something out of a bad disaster movie. Yes, that is definitely a row of little mushroom clouds indicating the deployment of tactical nuclear weapons all throughout the zone. I'm taking pictures and video for posterity in the hope that this madness can somehow be contained.

I'm making a mental note to talk with Valentin tomorrow to see if we can figure out how to maneuver into a link-up orbit before his supplies run out. I really don't think he is going to be resupplied anytime in the near future. I'll also have to calculate what the life expectancy will be for me, Stanley, and Valentin living together on good old *Lincoln One*.

I'm not an emotional type, so I don't really have anything profound to say at this moment.

"Yet another nice mess, indeed," I just said softly to Stanley as I scratch him under the chin. He continues to purr quietly as he lies strapped to my lap blissfully unaware of what I have just witnessed.

Thank God I prefer the company of cats.

ABOUT THE AUTHOR

Chris Sylvester has been an avid short story reader and writer since childhood. *Night Clouds* is his first published collection of short stories. His nonfiction work includes *Mouse Time!* and *The DC Capital Kids Family Guide to Washington, D.C.* Chris is also the creator of the thought-provoking website *Four-Choices.com*, which is available as a mobile app. Chris grew up in Maine and lives in Old Town Alexandria, Virginia.

www.ingramcontent.com/pod-product-compliance
Lightning Source LLC
Chambersburg PA
CBHW050926120626
46552CB00001B/66